UNEXPLODED
LOVE

by

PAUL GAIT

Grosvenor House
Publishing Limited

All rights reserved
Copyright © Paul Gait, 2015

The right of Paul Gait to be identified as the author of this
work has been asserted by him in accordance with Section 78
of the Copyright, Designs and Patents Act 1988

The book cover picture is copyright to Paul Gait

This book is published by
Grosvenor House Publishing Ltd
28-30 High Street, Guildford, Surrey, GU1 3EL.
www.grosvenorhousepublishing.co.uk

This book is sold subject to the conditions that it shall not, by way of
trade or otherwise, be lent, resold, hired out or otherwise circulated
without the author's or publisher's prior consent in any form of binding or
cover other than that in which it is published and
without a similar condition including this condition being imposed
on the subsequent purchaser.

This novel is entirely a work of fiction. The names, characters and
incidents portrayed in it are the work of the author's imagination. Any
resemblance to actual persons, living or dead, events or localities
is entirely coincidental.

A CIP record for this book
is available from the British Library

ISBN 978-1-78148-418-0

Thanks

To my wife Helen, for allowing me to spend countless hours to develop yet another story;

To family and friends, for continued support and encouragement.

To Janet for again spending many hours proof reading my manuscript.

Dedication

This book is dedicated to the Explosive Ordnance Disposal and de-mining teams around the world.

Chapter 1

2.45am Thursday June 1st 1944

The peace of the Belgium countryside was broken by the drone of large numbers of heavy bombers returning to England after night time bombing raids. Their missions had been to bomb the German transport infrastructure and attack enemy radar installations prior to the D – Day Normandy landings planned for 6th June.

A huge, four engine Halifax bomber is trailing behind the main body of aircraft. Closing in very quickly behind the lumbering giant are two Messerschmitt ME109 fighters, like sharks hunting their prey. The German fighters' speed and manoeuvrability are vastly superior to their target and they will surely take down the bomber like a 'sitting duck.

Desperately the pilot of the Halifax is wringing every bit of speed out of the Bristol Hercules engines. He knew within the formation of Lancaster bombers there would be an escort of Blenheim Mk IF night fighters which could offer protection.

It is a race against time as the 350 mph Messerschmitts hunt down their quarry. The Halifax is an unwieldy aircraft with a maximum speed of 200mph.

As they come in to range both pursuers start firing their MG 17 machine guns at the bomber. The shots do not find their target.

However, their high speed approach has already been spotted on the radar equipped Blenheims and four night fighters peel off from the formation to attack the two intruders.

Vastly outnumbered the German Me. 109 pilots make a hasty retreat and use every aerobatic manoeuvre to evade the formation's aerial bodyguards and make good their escape.

The mass formation of returning aircraft included planes which had taken part in large scale raids over Germany, France and Belgium. Also within the formation are two bombers from a small specialist raid on the vital railway network near the University town of Göttingen in Lower Saxony.

Although the Halifax is not damaged, many of the group in the formation are wearing the scars of battle. Some are clearly struggling, just limping home with smoking or failed engines. Gaping holes in wings and fuselage, rear gunner turrets smashed.

The Halifax pilot manoeuvred his heavy bomber into the back of the pack but struggled with the controls to keep his aircraft flying straight and level in the turbulence caused by the preceding planes.

After seeing off the Messerschmitts, two of the fighter escorts pulled along either side of the Halifax and checked it out.

However, strict radio silence, enforced on all ops, meant that no Morse code radio contact was undertaken with the newcomer. Instead, friendly gestures between the Halifax and fighter pilots reassured them of the integrity of the newcomer.

Although cold and mentally exhausted by their long nocturnal missions the crews summoned their final reserves to maintain a high level of surveillance against any potential threat.

To relax at this stage would be fatal. They had already survived attacks by enemy night fighters and the heavy defences surrounding their bombing targets.

As the formation approached the Ack-ack guns on the German Atlantic Wall coastal defences over Belgium the tension increased.

Fortunately tonight low cloud helped to hide their return to home shores and consequently very little flack came up to disrupt their homeward journey.

The long adrenaline fuelled hours dragged on but there was a growing anticipation that 'Lady Luck' had helped them survive yet another mission. The Lancaster crews silently prayed that the drone of the four Rolls-Royce Merlin engines would continue until they got home.

None of the airmen would admit that they were superstitious, but many crewmen secreted 'lucky mascots in their personal kit bags and went through exactly the same ritual on every mission in case the change of routine would compromise their luck.

Crews, hopeful but realistic, ticked off the obstacles to their safe return.

The next one was crossing the relatively short span of the English Channel without having to ditch.

Then, the final agonising part of their journey was to reach their home airfield hoping that Mother Nature wouldn't throw a last minute meteorological surprise of fog or gale force winds at them.

As they neared the English coast the formation split up and diverted to their various home airfields, relieved to have made it thus far.

Finally having survived all those major challenges, they hoped that the landing gear hadn't suffered any combat damage.

However, the newcomer had fallen back from the formation.

But the Halifax was still airworthy. It made the coast near Folkestone at low level. Coastal batteries and the ever watchful eyes and ears of the Royal Observer Corp recognised the unique sound of the Halifax. However they assumed that the plane was flying low because of battle damage.

The 'all seeing eye' of the newly developed microwave radar saw the Halifax crossing the coast. But the trackers lost sight of it on their screens as it lost altitude. Fighter command waited for the report of a plane down, but nothing came in and were much relieved to receive reports of a bomber heading west over Reading flying at low altitude.

Meanwhile, the plane quickly crossed southern England until it reached the Bristol Channel near Weston Super Mare. It then changed course and headed north following the meandering River Severn towards Gloucester startling early morning poachers illegally netting salmon as it zoomed over still at low altitude.

Near the spire of Gloucester cathedral it turned inland.

It was now 4.00am. In the distance the pilot could see a thin line of light sky as dawn backlit the Cotswold escarpment, the silhouette confirming his course.

The defence batteries near Barnwood tracked the passing aeroplane as it flew overhead but were reassured by the familiar sound of the four Bristol Hercules engines and assumed that its destination was the nearby Gloucester Aircraft Company airfield at Brockworth.

Their assumption proved right, but they were dismayed to subsequently hear the sound of explosions, which, they assumed, was the plane crash landing and setting off sympathetic explosions at the site.

However, the Halifax had not crashed but had deliberately dropped a string of delayed detonation high incendiary oil bombs on the factories and airfield.

One of their own dropping bombs on their home soil! Surely a mistake?

Confused by the unfolding events, the ack-ack battery surrounding the airdrome didn't fire on the 'friendly' aircraft, but watched open mouthed as the plane flew away and appeared to fly into the side of the Cotswold escarpment and explode in a fireball.

PART ONE

Getting to know you

Chapter 2

Present day

Frank strode along the corridor into the back bar of the Flying Machine pub, his Blackrock safety boots leaving a muddy trail of clay fragments behind him.

As he pushed open the black, gloss painted door into the public bar, he could see there were no other customers in the small room.

The bar furniture was sparse, but orderly. Chairs were neatly fitted under the round, varnished wooden tables. Four cardboard beer mats were neatly stacked in the centre of each table. There was a strong smell of paint about the place.

Behind the counter Liz looked up as the young man strode over to the bar.

'Pint of real ale, please,' he asked, feasting his eyes lustfully over her trim frame. 'Well now. I haven't seen you in here before,' he said, smiling.

'Likewise, and if you come in here again with dirty boots it will be the last time too,' she added, working the pull handle of the beer pump.

'Oh, I like a domineering woman. I bet those beer engines are good for improving the bust too,' he said, smiling.

'Do you mind? We don't want that sort of talk in here,' she said, indignantly.

'I was only going to say it's working, that's all,' he explained artfully.

'Look, do you want this pint in the glass or over your head?' she added.

'In the glass would be good, but whichever way you want to serve it is fine by me,' he teased.

'You're a bit cocky aren't you?' she said, continuing to concentrate on expertly filling the glass with the brown liquid.

'I have to say before I came in here, I was feeling a little off,' he confessed, 'but you definitely turned me on.'

'Are you Irish?' she asked, placing the filled glass in front of him.

'No. Why?'

'Well you're certainly full of the blarney.'

'Oh very good,' he said offering her a fiver held unconventionally between his index and middle fingers.

As she went to take it from him, he gripped her hand gently and said, 'Would you hold this for me while we go for a walk?'

'The only walking we'll be doing together will be to the pub door to eject you,' she added, slowly pulling her hand away.'

'Can I buy you a drink then, it's my birthday soon. We can celebrate together.'

'Well for your cheek I'll have a coffee, thank you. So where do you and your muddy boots come from?' she asked going to the till and depositing the money.

As he took a swig of beer he looked over the rim of his pint glass and gazed at her shapely figure and noted her long legs.

'We're doing some work on the site of the old Gloster Aircraft Company factory across the way, about half a mile away from here. I've been sat in a hot, sweaty JCB cab, digging holes all morning and felt in need of rehydrating myself.'

'What are they going to do over there after all these years?' she asked, returning opposite to him.

'Supposed to be the start of a big development, Retail Park, houses, roads, you name it.'

'I gather it's been a bit of an eyesore for years. Let's hope they've thought about the inevitable build-up of the traffic. It's a nightmare as it is without adding to the chaos,' she commented.

'Probably not. You know what these developers are like,' he said, supping his beer. 'Cram 'em in and maximise the profit. That's what it's all about.'

'How long's it likely to take?' she queried

'Oh I won't be here all that time. We're just preparing for surveying the ground works so the architects know what's there. Apparently the factory produced thousands of planes during the Second World War.'

'Really? What type of planes did they build?'

'Apparently it was Hurricanes and Typhoons.'

'Oh. It was obviously very important to the war effort then.'

'It was an old airfield too and they reckon that there is a warren of tunnels which they used during the war to go between the various factory buildings.'

'I suppose it must have had its fair share of bombing then.'

'Yeah, so we were told. Anyway enough of this old history,' he said perching on the bar stool. 'Lets' talk about something more interesting.'

'Such as?'

'You.'

'Oh here we go again.' Liz said, shaking her head in disbelief at his continued nonsense.

'Of all the many beautiful things about you, your smile is my favourite.' he added fixing her with a smile.

'You can do better than that surely?' she said returning his gaze.

'Let me guess what you do when you're not pulling pints. I bet you're a prima ballerina in between jobs.'

'Are you always like this with your corny chat up lines?'

'No I'm normally much more forward,' he quipped. 'Anyway, with beautiful long legs like that, you can't possible hide them serving behind the bar all day.'

Liz felt herself colour up. She hadn't experienced this level of compliments for years, for although she had lived on an army base; her husband's rank probably protected her from any ribald remarks.

At 35, Liz Witherton prided herself on her appearance. She spent an inordinate amount of time meticulously applying her makeup and looking after her distinctive shoulder length ginger hair. She was especially careful about choosing her clothes. It was retail therapy that kept her sane while husband William was serving the regiment as an Explosive Ordnance Disposal (EOD) officer.

'What's your name cheeky boy?' she asked.

'People call me Frank. But you can call me tonight,' he oozed.

To Liz's embarrassment and discomfort she saw Frank blatantly staring at her breasts. In fact, he was reading the name badge pinned on her polo shirt. 'If that boob's called Liz, what's the other one called?' he asked saucily.

'Yes very funny. As if I hadn't heard that one before a hundred times,' she rebuffed.

'Anyway, I think you're much too sophisticated to be merely a Liz. I think you're an Elizabeth,' he observed.

Embarrassed but liking the repartee, Liz moved away from the good-looking young man. There was an excitement building in her that she had not felt since she started dating William nearly fifteen years previously.

'Do you do food?' he asked putting his half empty beer glass down.

'Yes, here's the bar snack menu,' she said, handing it to him.

'What would you recommend?' he asked, ignoring it.

'Depends what you want,' she asked innocently without thinking.

'You know what I want?' he smoozed.

'When you're ready to order food, let me know,' she said trying to sound stern. So doing, she dropped the menu on the bar, turned away, poured herself a cup of coffee and started taking glasses out of the dishwasher, so that he couldn't see her embarrassment.

Frank picked up the list and quickly made his choice.

'If I can't have you for lunch, I'll just have to order a BLT on brown and a large bowl of cheesy chips please.'

'So that's where you get your cheesy chat up lines from is it?

'Oh, touché,' he said, smiling, pleased that she had returned his banter and looking forward to developing their relationship.

'That'll be £8:50 please,' she said holding out her hand. He dug a ten pound note out of his back pocket and offered it to her as before but she pulled her hand away before he could clutch it again.

She put the order through the till to the kitchen and gave him his change.

'So what do you do when you're not serving behind the bar?' he quizzed.

'Nothing that you would be interested in,' she said, still busying herself behind the bar, not wishing to divulge anything else about herself. 'What about you?'

'Oh I do a bit of 'keep fit' down at the gym and play rugby.'

'Yes, I could see that when you strutted into the bar.'

'Well if you've got a good body, you've got to flaunt it. Same as yourself,' he said flexing his biceps to reinforce the point.

'You can hardly say that I'm flaunting myself dressed in a black polo shirt and black slacks.'

'It depends on whose body that it's wrapped around. In your case it fits in all the right places,' he beamed, undressing her with his eyes.

Liz blushed again, for as much as she wanted to reject his compliments she was also feeling very flattered by them too.

In the kitchen the chef rang a bell to indicate the food was ready. Relieved to duck out of the full on raft of compliments Liz went through the small door behind the bar that led into the small kitchen.

'Busy out there?' the chef quizzed.

'No. Only one in at the moment. Trying to chat me up,' she added picking up the plate and bowl.

'Don't blame him. Why, if I was twenty years younger I'd…'

'Oh don't you start too. I shall be having you all for sexual harassment,' she laughed, backing out through the swing door into the bar.

'Oh that's a beautiful sight,' Frank said, watching her back her way into the bar.

'You are so full of it,' she replied putting the plate and bowl in front of him.

'I meant the food of course,' he added quickly. 'What else did you think I meant?'

'Of course,' she added, pink spots of embarrassment appearing on her cheeks, realising she had made a wrong assumption.

'Knife and fork?' he asked, smiling broadly, enjoying seeing her embarrassment.

She reached under the counter and presented him with the cutlery neatly wrapped in a white paper serviette.

'I hesitate to ask if you want anything else?' she said, 'knowing where your mind is.'

'My heart and mind are yours, you know that,' he said falsely, 'but could I have some salt in the meantime, please?'

'Is the job going to be long?' she asked putting the salt pot from under the counter in front of him, keen to change the subject.

'Yeah, a couple months I reckon,' he muttered his mouth full of BLT and spraying a few breadcrumbs as he spoke. 'Oh excuse me, 'he added, 'I'm spitting my food at you.'

'Well, he has some manners after all,' she thought. 'You'll get indigestion if you gobble your food like that.'

'Yes, Mum,' he mocked. 'Bloody hell, is that the time? Talking to you time stood still. I got to get back to the job otherwise my partner will be whinging.'

He took a handful of chips and stuffed them into his mouth.

'Why so long if you're not actually building anything?'

He swallowed the chips quickly. 'The place was apparently bombed during the Second World War and we're checking the bomb survey to make sure it's all safe.'

'Oh, so does that mean I will have to put up with your cheek for all that time.'

'If you're lucky and play your cards right,' he said, draining his pint glass.

He got up off the stool and made his way purposefully to the door.

'See you tomorrow…Elizabeth,' he added, beaming.

'So long as your boots are clean,' she shouted as he closed the door. Disappointed that a bright part of her day had just left. She cleared up his empty plate, bowl and pint glass. The place suddenly felt depressing.

Chapter 3

Afghanistan

'Make us a brew Smithy,' William asked his number two as they returned from a shout. 'I'm parched.'

The officer gently put the large clear polythene evidence bag on the table and gazed at the components of the Improvised Explosive Device (IED) he'd just defused.

'You know, I think we've got a new bomb maker on our patch. I've not seen one like this before,' he shouted to his assistant.

'I swear it's getting hotter out there you know,' he added, as he removed his helmet and body armour. He unpeeled his sweat soaked tee shirt and wiped his back and chest down with the soft material.

'Boss, there's a message for you,' Smithy said, handing his officer a folded piece of paper.

William took the paper and looked at it briefly. 'Oh good, Pete's coming over for a chat. That'll be just right to discuss todays little find,' he said, looking at the contents of the bag. 'We need to catch this one before he gets too confident.

Pete was William's mentor, also an Ammunition Technical Officer (ATO). He had years of IED experience and had taken William under his wing as soon as he arrived in Afghanistan. They'd spent many valuable hours together to bring William up to speed on the tactics and anti-tamper methods that the bomb makers used.

'We'll do the forensic report later, Smithy. Go and take five.

'OK boss. Let me know when you want to reconvene.'

The sergeant left the tent and headed back to his own.

'He's a good man,' thought William. 'He should make a good ATO.'

William's tent served as a home, office and his bedroom. He had a few personal items around but kept Liz's picture in a drawer which he only looked at occasionally. 'No good pining for what you can't have,' Pete had advised. 'She's already in your head and presumably in your heart so don't compromise your life by thinking about her on ops.'

William had taken his words to heart and removed all reminders of home from sight.

Today, however, he took out the photo and gazed at the smiling face. He lay on his cot still holding the framed picture and was immediately transported back to the day he had taken it.

They were on honeymoon in the warm West Indies island of St Kitts. It was nirvana with the clear blue sky, white sand and the azure blue sea. They had been drinking rum cocktails starting just after breakfast. They were not drunk, just blissfully happy. The world outside had stopped. They were in paradise. Her beautiful smile lit up her face and undermined his normal stoic emotions. His heart fluttered. He was in love. He was so lucky. She was his partner, his wife, his life.

Suddenly there was a voice.

'Had a busy morning, William?' the gentle voice asked.

William stirred. He had dozed off, still holding the photograph. Quickly realising what he was holding, he slid it back into the drawer and swung his feet off his cot.

'Hello Pete,' he said standing, and vigorously shaking the others hand. 'Not particularly, no. Sit down. I'll get you a brew. Mine's probably cold now.'

The other did as he was bid and sat next to the 'office' table.

'It's nice to see you. To what do I owe the pleasure?' William asked busying himself making his visitor a cup of tea.

'Thought we ought to have a catch up with things and I've got some news.' Pete said in his soft West Country accent. His gentle sing-song voice pervaded peace and calm which made him appear to be 'laid back' and able to handle any amount of stress when others around him were panicking. His team had even pinned up a banner in his 'office'. '*When others around you are losing their heads, you obviously don't know what the f... is going on.*'

He'd laughed when he saw it, modestly acknowledging that he had stopped a few people from losing it, in times of stress, usually under fire.

'I see you've bagged another toy,' Pete said, picking up the evidence bag and turning it around to examine its contents through the plastic. 'Usual components I see. Ah now that's interesting,' he said bringing the bag closer to his face

'What's that? I haven't started the forensic report yet,' William informed him, putting the two large mugs of tea on the table.

'See the way he terminates the wire before he solders it?' Pete said, lifting the bag to William's face.

'Yes. It's wound around the tag twice and then overlapped before being cut off,' he added looking at the other. 'Neat job!'

'I've seen this on a few that I've done recently. It looks like we've got a new 'factory' churning these out.'

'Got any fingerprint or DNA results back yet?'

'No nothing yet. Although usually it's not the maker's anyway. He's too clever to be caught like that. Uses rubber gloves I expect. No. Any prints we get are usually from the 'cannon fodder' that has the job of laying them.'

Pete put the bag gently back on the table.

'Well, pretty soon we won't be caring anyway,' he said, picking up his mug of tea.

'Why's that?' William asked, puzzled.

'We've got the dates for our final withdraw.'

'Really?'

'Yes. End of the month.'

'Really! As soon as that. I know that they've been shipping the stuff off for months now, but I thought we'd be here until all our guys were out.'

'No, the Ruperts have decided.'

'Or is it politically motivated?'

'Well, yes you're right. It's the politicians that pull the strings after all.'

'So we might never know who matey, the new bomber is then?'

'No. But then again the Afghans have to take on our role. Most of them are pretty good. Unfortunately, those that aren't, are not ATOs for very long. Sadly the mortality rate is pretty high,' he said quietly.

'Yes, and, they've lost some good people too.'

'Well I'll miss this,' Pete mused reflectively. 'I shall have to go back to playing chess instead.'

'Chess is a damn sight less dangerous though. I'll go back to my Regiment and back to civilian clearance I expect.' William added.

He thought about the contrasts between Afghanistan and the UK. Here it was new, cutting age technology with components mostly in prime condition in the baking heat. Whereas, at home, it would be muddy holes with rusty corroding ordnance with an unpredictable handling outcome. Both still required nerves of steel and a high degree of respect for their designers.

He would miss his injection of daily 'excitement'. Still, some of the World War Two bombs could be challenging, although there was a greater tendency to explode them in situ if possible.

'What were you dreaming about when I arrived? You were smiling inanely, wherever you were,' Pete asked.

'Well I never dream normally. But I was back on honeymoon in the West Indies.' William replied.

'Obviously time for you to get back home and see the wife then.'

William smiled. He was already thinking of their reunion.

Chapter 4

Liz had finished her lunch time shift early as there were few customers. As she was in no great hurry, she drove the back roads from the Flying Machine to her home in Cheltenham skirting the bottom of Churchdown Hill, enjoying driving through the blossoming spring countryside. She was glad of the air conditioning as her dashboard display indicated an unseasonably hot 24 degrees outside.

The traffic was light until she entered Cheltenham. However within twenty minutes of leaving the pub she arrived in Lansdown Crescent where she lived. After parking her car in her designated spot she descended the worn stone steps to her basement flat and unlocked the door. As she stepped in she was greeted by the relative coolness that the basement flat provided. She threw her car keys on to the small shelf by the door and picked up the mail from the floor. As she straightened up she caught sight of herself in the long mirror on the far wall and gazed at the reflection that stared back at her.

She swivelled around and admired her left side profile, checking the lines of her 34 inch bust flowing down to her flat stomach, her long legs and the contour of her pert bottom. She then pirouetted the other way and re-checked her right side profile. She liked what she saw.

'Mmm, well perhaps I am trim for a thirty five year old,' she said, piling her long hair up and pouting at the mirror. The encounter with Frank had really buoyed her flagging self-esteem.

She examined the mail. There was no envelope bearing William's neat handwriting. No anniversary card then. She opened the door to see if she had overlooked the bouquet that he normally sent. Nothing.

Disappointed, she stepped back in to the flat and spotted the flashing message light on the answer machine. Perhaps William had called to wish her happy anniversary instead. She pressed the play button in great anticipation but was saddened not to hear his voice. It was instead her friend Mel asking if she fancied going to a dance. She decided she would call her back later.

Understandably, William had asked her not to call him 'at work' unless it was a dire emergency. Instead, he said he would initiate the call when he wanted to chat to her. But the occasions were few and far between.

She tried to down play her disappointment. 'It wasn't an important anniversary anyway,' she thought. 'I'm sure he's doing something important.'

Rather than dwell on the missing call, card and bouquet, she decided to go for a run in spite of the mini 'heatwave', unusual for May. Quickly she slipped out of her 'day clothes' and donned her running kit.

As she exited the flat she again checked herself in the mirror. She looked good dressed in her fashionable short sleeve black running top with matching black three quarter length tights, both trimmed with pink side flashes. She felt confident about herself and looked every bit a plausible athlete.

She recalled Frank's comments about her long legs. The black tights certainly made her legs look even longer. He had been right about her being a dancer, for choreography had been an integral part of her university drama course.

She put her hair in a ponytail and tamed it further with a stylish broad pink headband edged with black, matching her top and tights.

Finally she grabbed her strange looking elliptical drinks bottle which always reminded her of a large plastic knuckleduster and filled it with cold water from the tap.

She had started running at University, initially because she fancied William and it was a way of getting to know the quiet individual. However during her post degree days she maintained her interest in William and running. Subsequently they got married and she had become a running junkie taking to the streets at least three times a week. It also kept her weight down and her overall fitness up.

Her normal run from home was just less than 7 kilometres around the pavements of Cheltenham, which usually took about 45 minutes. It was an almost flat street run which she enjoyed, although waiting to cross the roads disrupted her routine and sometimes added up to fifteen minutes to her time.

However, she felt relaxed and safe in these genteel tree lined roads and harboured no fears of running around the beautiful Regency town.

Liz checked she had locked the front door and put the key in a small Velcro pocket of her running top. Pulling herself up the short metal railings that guarded the drop into the basement, she climbed up the stone steps.

She crossed the road into the park area opposite and using the small wooden bench and picnic table, did her routine of warm up stretching exercises.

Finally, she started her run through the park where thousands of daisies formed a random pattern in the carpet of manicured grass.

Her run took her along the semi-circular tree lined road in front of the massive convex shaped four storey structure of the Lansdown Crescent.

The frontage of every honeycomb terraced house was identical with wide stone steps leading to the ground floor flats. At the top of the steps, supported on four massive Cotswold stone pillars were decorative stone porches.

An intricate necklace of wrought iron railings ran along the face of the building providing safety barriers for first floor balconies.

Geometrically aligned sash windows adorned the front of the terrace, each with twelve square panes providing light into the small flats. Sub dividing most windows, a cascade of neatly tied net curtains provided a tantalising glimpse into their inner sanctum.

Like Liz's, each property also had small self-contained basement flat accessed down a short flight of stone steps. Metal railings guarded the six foot drop into the basement.

A five foot manicured privet hedge bordered the periphery of the whole convex sweep of the colossal building.

Liz emerged from the quiet crescent to cross the busy main road by the ornamental lamp standard with its triple drop globe lamps and made her way into Montpellier Terrace. She could see marquees for an outdoor exhibition laid out between the lovingly tended flower borders of the large park area in Montpellier Gardens and could hear the excited squeals of children in the play area.

She had never thought of becoming a mother, for with William's occupation as an Explosive Ordnance Disposal officer it was a topic they didn't even discuss.

The much disliked 161 feet of the 1960's high rise lozenge shaped multi-storey Eagle Star building came into view. It had been a contentious building throughout its history; certainly a blot on the landscape and totally out of place in the low rise area of Cheltenham.

Jogging on the spot, waiting to cross the busy A46 Bath Road, she saw the brown tourist sign for the Everyman theatre. Like the Cheltenham playhouse she frequented both theatres, often building scenery, helping back stage and occasionally 'treading the boards.' Although she had a drama degree she enjoyed dancing more than acting and rarely went for auditions.

Finally the lights changed and she ran across into Sandford Road with the Cathedral looking Cheltenham College chapel set back on the corner. She always felt good when she saw the ancient buildings, a source of permanence in an uncertain world, proudly claiming to have been educating young people since 1841.

Further along Sandford road she heard the sounds of a busy grass cutting machine and behind it the quaintly English sight of men in whites playing college cricket. The sound of leather on willow echoed across the field above the industrious grass cutter.

Her run took her past the side of the strange mix of rectangular and colonnaded buildings which housed the west wing of Cheltenham General hospital. This always reminded her of the dangerous occupation in which William was involved. They had spoken many times about his choice of work. The risks of him being killed or severely injured were always foremost in her thoughts. She doubted she would have the courage to cope with the demands of a severely injured husband.

Their discussions always came back to the same point. He enjoyed the buzz and excitement of beating the enemy's effort to kill and maim.

'It's like a deadly game of chess and I have to win, otherwise...' he never said the words but they both knew what he meant. 'You worrying won't help me. You've just got to put my welfare to the back of your mind.' He'd always said to placate her.

She shook her head to erase the black thoughts.

Initially, she'd lived in fear of the dreaded 'knock on the door' by uniformed personnel, harbingers of bad news. It had taken time not to get tense when someone called at the door. Eventually she'd come to terms with it. However, sadly, their loving relationship lost the closeness of their early romance as a result.

She really enjoyed being outdoors in May. Everything was bursting into life.

Although the fresh leaf cover made the overhanging branches heavy forcing her duck under them as she ran, the new foliage waving a greeting as it swayed gently in the warm light breeze. Even the tall hedges lining the pavements wore their new spring 'clothes'.

Liz felt good as she approached the sign that said Cox's Meadow, Oxford A40. She took a swig out of her drinks bottle resisting the temptation to drop into the Meadow café for a cooling ice cream. Here too was another reminder of why she loved living in

Cheltenham for in front of her was another wide swathe of manicured parkland behind which the beautiful outline of the Cotswold escarpment glowed in the afternoon sunshine.

Liz ran along the short stretch of the A40 which also signposted the Station and Staverton Airport. Her thoughts went back to a brief walking holiday she'd had with William when they'd flown from the small local airport to the Isle of Man on board a small twin engine turboprop. The plane was so noisy that the inflight films were old silent movies with subtitles. The film was projected on to one screen behind the pilot. She chuckled to herself at the recollection. That had been a nice break in between William's tours but he was still tense and never really let himself relax.

Liz's thoughts went back to her own health as she passed the Breast Cancer Unit which always reminded her to check herself for lumps while she showered. She shuddered at the thought of finding something.

Just as she got to a high walled Cheltenham College building a car pulled up on the other side of the narrow road and started matching her speed. She felt a moment of panic. She'd read only recently about East European gangs kidnapping women off the streets.

If it had only pulled up a few minutes earlier she could have escaped down a side road. But the road was now deserted so no-one would see what was going on. She tried to think what to do. Her mind overwhelmed with apprehension. She increased her pace.

The car did likewise. She was starting to panic inside. If the occupant tried anything, her screams would surely echo off walls and someone from the cricket pitch would come to her rescue. Wouldn't they?

The car beeped its horn and someone waved. She ignored it. In her peripheral vision she could see that the car was still keeping pace with her. Perhaps they only wanted directions. She resisted the temptation to look and increased her pace. The car increased speed to keep abreast of her. She was starting to feel threatened and wondering what to do when the driver called.

'Hey Leggy Liz,' the voice said. She continued running, trying to ignore the kerb crawler.

The horn again.

Her curiosity got the better of her. She quickly glanced across at the car. It was a Renault 19. The driver lifted his sunglasses. Instantly she recognised the face. It was Frank, the flirty pub customer.

'I thought it was you,' he shouted, alternating his gaze from her to the road. 'Couldn't mistake those legs and your cute bum.'

'God, you gave me such a fright.' Liz said putting her hand over her wildly beating heart.

'Sorry about that. Did you think I was stalking you?'

'Yes. Oh. I'm all of a flutter,' she said, flapping her hand in front of her hot face.

'Do you live over here then?' he queried.

'Yes,' she shouted, slowing her pace slightly and feeling relieved that her fears of abduction were unfounded.

Before they could strike up any more of a conversation, a Police car pulled right behind Frank's car and eyed him suspiciously. Frank took the hint and accelerated. 'I'll see you in the pub tomorrow,' he shouted over his shoulder as he sped off.

The Police driver wound down his window and asked 'Is he bothering you Miss?'

'No, it's OK Officer I know him. But thanks.'

'OK, enjoy your run.' And so saying he drove off too.

'Thanks,' she called breathlessly as the patrol car accelerated down the road.

This time, the pedestrian lights were with her as she again crossed the busy A46 near the other side of the spectacular Cheltenham College buildings and entered Suffolk Road.

As she ran further on, she half expected to see Frank parked by the wide road at Tivoli Circus and waiting for her. She was mildly disappointed that he wasn't there.

Seeing the road sign for Tivoli Circus reminded her of a childhood trip to London with her parents to see the famous Piccadilly Circus. She was very upset and had cried her eyes out when she discovered there was no big Circus Tent or clowns as she'd expected. She chuckled at the memory.

Pausing briefly to wait for a gap in the traffic, Liz carried on across the famous Rotunda Island with its busy filling station and, resisting the temptation to go for a drink in the Lansdown pub, she ran into Queens Road.

Eventually, she coasted a small incline at the end of the road and could see the sign for the surprisingly small two platform Cheltenham Spa railway station. The clientele of the small station had changed over the years. Initially it had been Victorian passengers coming to drink the Spa water, whereas nowadays it's the annual 'Irish invasion' arriving for Gold Cup week, drinking most town bars dry.

She had collected William from here several times while he was doing his two year-long training for his current job. She could see him changing during it. He became more and more reserved as the intensity of the training increased. It was a testing time for their relationship.

She ran down the pedestrian walkway by the side of Honeybourne Way separating the pedestrians from the traffic, glad to get away from the busy Gloucester Road and alongside the diminutive, brook like River Chelt for a short distance.

Her feet were hot in her trainers and she noticed her pace had dropped. She stopped and took a drink from her water bottle and poured the rest over her head and the back of her neck. She gasped as it cascaded down between her breasts and pooled at her waist briefly.

'Come on Elizabeth,' she goaded. 'Nearly there.'

She got her rhythm back and ran light footed past Christ Church and the sports centre where children were noisily playing tennis.

Her legs were hot as she ran back into an area of honeycomb four storey terrace houses similar to but not as majestic as the Crescent.

'Nearly there,' she panted.

Then finally back to the Crescent itself where she could see people picnicking on the grassy area near the children's play area.

She checked her watch and was pleased with her run time. In spite of slowing down to talk to Frank, she'd met her target.

After Liz had completed her post run recovery regime; she opened the door of her flat and grabbed a bottle of ice cold water from the refrigerator and went back outside, removing her headband and scrunchie as she did so. She sat on the warm, top basement step and shook her head to untangle her ponytail. Although she was hot and sweaty, she felt the wonderful buzz that she always experienced after a run.

She put the cold bottle to her forehead and pulse spots of her wrists immediately feeling the cooling effects.

After rehydrating herself and cooling down for a few minutes she went back in to the flat stripped off her sweat soaked clothes and stepped into the 'p' shaped bath which doubled as a shower.

Setting the temperature to cool, she luxuriated in the stinging jets of water for ten long minutes cooling herself before soaping. Feeling refreshed, she stepped out of the bath and towelled herself down. She wrapped her long wet hair in a towel shaped turban, lay on her bed and dozed off in the warm flat.

Unlike William's dream of their West Indies honeymoon, Liz's dream was of a close encounter in the hot cab of Frank's JCB.

Chapter 5

Afghanistan

William had other things on his mind that prevented him making the call to wish Liz happy anniversary. Normally he would have got some flowers sent to her, but even that had been forgotten in the 'heat of battle'.

Intelligence had been received about the location of a bomb factory and an early morning raid was planned. William's team were to be an integral part of the raid to ensure any booby traps or IEDs were quickly dealt with so that the raid could be executed quickly.

He had briefed the team about their involvement in the operation and went through the plans several times checking that everyone knew their role.

At the agreed time, the Infantry Platoon and EOD team were transported to within a half mile of their target before they disembarked.

For William the first five metres after stepping out of the protection of the Warthog armoured vehicle was always a heart stopping moment. The anticipation of whether they'd been spotted and being targeted by a hidden sniper was gut wrenching. Would they hear the crack of a gun? Would the shout of 'man down' as a bullet found its deadly mark abort the mission before it had even started?

Nothing happened. They hadn't been compromised. William breathed a sigh of relief. The desert air was still.

The group were led by a soldier with a mine detector methodically sweeping the path ahead. They walked quietly in single file ten metres apart, everyone using their night vision goggles to probe the desert darkness.

The clandestine operation was being coordinated through an airborne command centre flying at high altitude. Nearby, a heavily armed drone was circling in a holding pattern ready to be deployed if required, to target the insurgents with its hellfire missiles.

Aerial surveillance came from a high tech camera locked on the target building. In addition, the latest infrared technology identified the location of the insurgent guards protecting the bomber's store.

On his screen the camera surveillance operator could make out the ghostly green images of the patrol heading towards the building and had located the immobile Taliban guards who were well placed around the periphery of the target building.

The command plane was in direct contact with the Infantry Captain leading the raid.

'Raider1. This is Skyhawk. Your first guard is at your two o'clock, two hundred metres.'

The Captain raised his hand and signalled to his patrol to stop. He pointed in the 'two o'clock' direction and all the members of the patrol lifted their rifles and gazed through their night sights to seek out the insurgent.

'Target acquired,' he heard one of them say.

Not wishing to warn the other guards of their approach, he nominated two of the patrol to remain on station and target the guard.

Rules of engagement meant they weren't allowed to fire until fired upon. A rule he thought crazy. It was typical of a policy written from behind the safety of a desk, thousands of miles away.

Slowly, the rest of the platoon moved forward hugging the rugged brick wall of the compound.

'Your next guard is in front of the building,' the aerial guardian's calm voice informed him.

Again the Leader signalled to halt and gestured to the soldier carrying a short ladder that he should put it against the wall and lead a few others over.

'Be aware Raider 1 that guard 2 is likely to see you scaling the wall. Suggest you are prepared, over.'

'Roger that.'

Quickly the Leader passed on the message and instructed the soldier to wait at the top of the ladder for further instructions. He then led the remaining group further along until they reached the edge of the building situated on the other side of the wall. He signalled for William to come forward to stick C4 plastic explosives to blow a hole in the wall.

'Skyhawk. Any movement?'

'Negative. The guards are still immobile.'

William carefully stuck the explosive to the wall and ran a short length of detonation wire back to a hand held firing unit held by Smithy.

'Hopefully there isn't anything the other side of the wall that will generate a secondary explosion,' he whispered.

He looked at the Infantry Captain for permission to proceed. The Captain duly checked that the troops were far enough away from the site and gave the thumbs up.

William put his hand up with his five fingers spread open. He held it to Smithy and counted down by retracting one finger at a time.

After what seemed an age, Skyhawk could see the soldiers moving away from the building and heard the Leader also counting down.

'Five, four, three, two, one.' Quickly he turned off the high intensity viewer to ensure that the explosion didn't 'burn out' the electronics. Nevertheless, he saw the explosion and quickly turned it back on again after a few seconds.

On the screen he could see the action as the team rushed through the still smoking hole in the wall.

Alerted by the explosion he could see the Taliban guards now firing and saw the return fire from the soldiers. Unsure of what was going on, the other three guards hesitated briefly, and then took to their heels.

'Raider 1 this is Skyhawk. Your other opponents have fled. No other heat sources detected.'

'Skyhawk, Raider 1 Roger that. Keep an eye out for us. I'm sure the fireworks will have attracted a lot more attention. Over.'

'Roger Wilco.'

Skyhawk could see the soldiers emerging from the front of the building and taking up defensive positions.

William remained with his team outside the building until it had been thoroughly searched for anyone hiding inside. After five minutes the infantry man beckoned him forward.

'I think we've won the jackpot,' the Leader said smiling, as William joined him.

'Have a look at that,' he said, shining his torch around the smoke and dust laden room.

The torch revealed an Aladdin's cave of bomb making material. Large numbers of various types of mobile phones, a stack of detonators, wiring tools, printed circuit boards, batteries, coils of multicolour insulated wire, and rolls of insulating tape were all piled high on a table.

On the floor nearby were several ordnance shells and old soviet landmines. In another part of the room there was a neat pile of blocks of homemade explosive wrapped in polythene sheets. Each block was secured by black insulating tape with insulated connecting wires trailing out of the polythene.

In a cupboard nearby there was a pile of circuit drawings, a collection of AK47s and ammunition lay scattered over the floor.

Pinned to the wall, a map of the local area caught William's eye. On closer examination he noted that it was annotated with various pencil marks, presumably identifying the location of IEDs planted or planned.

'Brilliant. This will make my job easier,' he said, carefully removing it from the wall and rolling it up.

'It looks like a training school for novice bomb makers.' William said smiling. 'This will stop the bastards for a little while. Do all your guys know not to touch anything until I have made sure it's not booby trapped?' he asked switching on his high intensity headlamp.

'Yes,' the infantry officer replied.

'Ok. I'll leave you to secure the area. In the meantime I'll photograph this lot and we'll get some transport here to get it back to base,' William said smiling. 'We can log it all there in peace. It will give us time to look for any clues as to who our man is.'

'One up to us,' the Infantry Captain said, gleefully. 'Is that right they found one of these bomb makers in the UK?'

'Yes. He thought he was safe but they got him from the forensics he'd left on the components.'

'No hiding place eh? Anyway getting hold of this lot will save a few lives for sure.'

'Yes, but sadly only until they re-establish their supply lines,' William added realistically.

Chapter 6

Liz looked out of the pub window. The rain was still bucketing down as it had done all night. The unseasonal early heatwave had ended in an equally unseasonal thunderstorm.

Few people were venturing out because of the downpour and the morning was dragging on. She had already done her usual tidying up in the pub and had even started the Sudoku to while away the hours.

Liz thought at least Frank's arrival would brighten up her day. She was looking forward to seeing him again for there was something in him she found exciting. She particularly liked his cheeky banter and infectious smile. He was, after all, quite handsome and more importantly, interested in her.

Liz kept clock watching every few minutes. Every time the door opened she hoped it was him and disappointed when he failed to emerge. Like an anxious dog waiting for its owner to return she kept looking expectantly at the door. When it came to the end of her shift and he hadn't shown, she felt quite disheartened, mortified that he hadn't arrived.

The day got worse for her for when she got home she discovered her basement had flooded. The drains, dodgy at the best of times, had been unable to cope with the deluge and had backed up into concrete area in front of her flat. Some had leaked over the top of her raised threshold and into her flat.

'Damn it. Just right to cap the end of a depressing day,' she muttered to herself.

Although it wasn't a significant amount of water, nevertheless she spent the rest of the afternoon and evening mopping up. Her carpet was ruined so she decided she needed to get the drains sorted.

Chapter 7

However the weather had improved the following day and when the pub door opened at lunch time she was elated to see Frank's tall figure standing in the doorway, in his hand, a pair of muddy boots.

'I daren't upset you by wearing my dirty boots again Mum,' he said smiling.

'That's a good boy,' she replied, feeling excited to see him and getting back into the spirit of their banter. 'Now if you're a good boy Mummy will allow you to have…'

'A kiss?' Frank interrupted, beaming.

'Not a chance,' she added quickly, colouring up. 'But I'll allow you to buy a pint.'

Frank dropped his boots near the doorway. 'Spoilsport!' he blurted pretending to be upset.

'Anyway were you stalking me in Cheltenham the other day?' she demanded.

'No. But I wish I had. I was on my way to see the boss. He'd got a weather report about the thunderstorm yesterday so he wanted to plan an alternative job for me just in case. No rest for the wicked, eh!'

'Oh, is that why you weren't in yesterday?'

'Yeah. Did you miss me?'

'No,' she lied.

'Pity. I missed you,' he said giving her one of his beaming smiles.

She fidgeted uncomfortably under his gaze.

'Unfortunately, we did some maintenance work on the drains back at base,'' he continued.

'Oh that's interesting. I've got trouble with my drains,' she said innocently.

'Have you seen your doctor about it?' he joked.

'You know what I mean. You fool. I got home yesterday and it had flooded the front of my flat and leaked in.'

'Much damage?'

'Yes I spent all afternoon and evening drying it off. I think my carpets ruined.'

'Insurance job then?'

No, it's happened before and they won't insure me. It's a basement flat.'

'Oh dear. I could come and have a look at your drains if you want me to,' he offered.

For a moment she was flummoxed. 'I...I'm...' She was now getting in too deep. She would have to give him her address. Flirting in the bar was OK but...

'Well think about it. The offer is there if you want me to try and sort it out for you.'

'That's very kind, thanks.'

' 'We knew that the heavy rain would make the ground very sodden. When it's like that it's impossible to operate the JCB safely,' he added.

'You mean, that's why you were skiving.' She jested.

'No, I wasn't. It's because the groundwater doesn't drain very well.' He became serious. 'There are some boggy bits on the site and the rain would have made it impossible to work. As it is, it's still pretty marshy there today.

'Oh dear. Well you'll be gutted to know that you missed out on the free beer,' she teased.

'Free beer? That's a bummer. Can I have mine today then?

'No. Sorry. The special offer lasted only one day to attract the crowds in because of the rain.'

'Drat. But I can't imagine the Landlord giving anything away.'

'No, you're right he didn't. So what's it to be today?'

'Oh you tease,' he said sitting on the barstool opposite. 'With suggestive questions like that you set my imagination running wild.'

'If you can keep your mind off sex for a minute,' she insisted.

'Me talk about sex? You do me a disservice,' he pleaded with false innocence.

'So, what's it to be?'

'Ein bier bitte.'

'Oh get you. Is there no end to your talents? 'So you can talk German as well as English and bullshit.'

'Elizabeth, that's not the sort of language I expect to hear from a refined lady such as yourself,' he blurted in mock horror.

'It's obviously rubbing off from you,' she reposted.

'Oh that's hurtful,' he said, with feigned distress. 'Actually it's no big deal for me speaking German. My family comes from Germany.'

'Oh proper European then!' she stated, moving towards the beer pump. 'Pint of real ale then?'

'Yes please.'

Frank watched closely as Liz pulled his pint, admiring the fine down on her sun bronzed arm which caught the light. Her small hands grasping the beer engine handle made him feel weak inside. He studied her face. Total concentration as she filled the beer mug, the tip of her tongue flicking sensuously over her lips.

'You have an exquisite technique pulling that beer pump,' he said huskily. 'You know what it reminds me of?' he added, seductively.

'Food?' She demanded ignoring the innuendo.

'Another of those delicious BLT's will do me nicely thanks.'

Frank fished a crumpled ten pound note from his back pocket and offered it to Liz in outstretched fingers. She took it slowly and was pleased to have her small hand sandwiched between his large hard hands.

'Got you,' he said smiling.

'You'll have to let me go otherwise I can't give you any change,' she replied, without trying to pull away, a slight quiver in her voice.

'Holding your hand is change enough,' he beamed. Reluctantly he let go. Liz went to the til and rang up his order. She could feel his eyes on her as she fished around the coin drawer for his change and felt excited by his attention.

'Right Sir, your food order will be with you shortly,' she said returning to him. She dropped the coins into his open palm and as she did so, he enfolded both his hands around hers again. She felt a flutter of excitement in her stomach but slowly pulled her hand away from the brief 'embrace'. All the while he had been studying the reaction on her face.

He cleared his throat, 'I didn't realise you were a runner,' he said, picking up his pint glass. 'No wonder you're in good shape.'

'Thank you kind Sir,' she blushed. 'I've been running for a few years now.'

'Is that so nobody can catch you and chat you up?' he probed.

'In any case, I'm...' she stopped in mid-sentence for she was struck by a crazy notion. For the first time in her married life she wanted to hide the fact that she had a husband. Hoping that he hadn't already spotted her wedding ring, she excused herself by saying, 'I'm just going to check on your food order.'

'Ok,' he said, watching her closely as she disappeared into the kitchen.

Instead of staying in the kitchen she went to the staff toilet, licked the flesh of her ring finger to make it slippery and started tugging at the small gold band.

'What the hell are you doing?' she chided herself, stopping and gazing at her reddened finger. 'Look at you. Throwing yourself at a bloke almost half your age?'

She thought about the differences between William and Frank's personalities. They were poles apart.

Frank exuded a 'joie de vie', had energy, and a happy go lucky nature. His cheerful chat up lines made her laugh. When he was talking to her he was totally focussed on her. She was flattered by it. She didn't have to fight anyone else for his attention. Like a giddy school girl, he made her feel important.

Whereas William was a controlled and staid individual. Although their personalities worked well together, in reality the relationship had become dull, predictable, even boring. Almost like brother and sister. The excitement had gone out of their marriage

She had to admit that he hadn't always been like that. He'd been a fun guy when she first met him. But his job had changed him to a serious, emotionally flat person.

She thought about the lack of their togetherness. In the early days separation through his various postings didn't seem to matter. But now, somehow it did. She wanted to be fussed over, to be complemented, to be loved, to be touched, stroked, and hugged. Disappointingly, William's 'reserved' romance failed to excite her anymore.

She tried to rationalise it. Ok, William was doing a vital job for Queen and country in fifty degree heat in a hostile country. Were he was forever looking over his shoulder dodging bombs and bullets. Frank, on the other hand, was digging holes in an air conditioned JCB with no threats or danger. But even so...

But with Frank she was experiencing something different, this other man's attention excited her.

She was working herself into a frenzy of dissatisfaction. To add to her discontent she didn't even have a 'decent' house to live in. They had rented out their own fully furnished house. On the rare occasions William came home from a tour he stayed with her in the flat and frustratingly got under her feet. He was constantly messing up her well-ordered meticulously planned daily routine.

She shook her head to clear her mind of her marital negativity. However, she gave the ring one last tug and this time it came off. She quickly put it into her pocket and made her way back to the kitchen where Frank's food was waiting.

She picked up the plate and took it to him in the bar.

'I thought you'd deserted me,' he said, looking into her eyes, trying to read her thoughts.

'Sorry about the wait,' she said, fishing out the cutlery from under the bar and presenting it to him. 'Sauces? Don't tell me. Tomato wasn't it?'

'You're getting to know what I like. Well some of what I like anyway,' he added seductively, throwing her a beaming smile. He picked up the BLT in his thick chipolata sized fingers and demolished a large portion in one enormous bite.

'You running again this afternoon?' he asked, spraying crumbs.

'Yes. I normally do alternate days. Keeps me fit,' she announced putting her hand on her flat stomach.

'So I can see,' he added, following her hand with lustful eyes. 'Well fit,' he whispered, smirking.

'You obviously keep fit too. Is that in the gym?'

'Bit of gym. Bit of circuit training. I'm playing in a big rugby game in a few days. You can come and watch me perform if you like. On the pitch of course,' he added suggestively.

'Of course, where else? No I'm sorry but I'm busy at weekends painting scenery for our next show.'

'You can paint me in my rugby gear if you like. I do modelling.'

'I paint with a nine inch roller,' she explained.

'Well that will cover one part of me at least,' he added cheekily.

Liz blushed at the innuendo, 'Oh hark at you big boy,' she laughed, trying to play down his boast.

'I'm nothing but honest,' he said, washing down the BLT with the last drop of his pint.

'Anyway, as much as I'd like to stay with you all afternoon and as you aren't going to invite me back to your boudoir, I shall have to get back to digging holes.'

'Umm, I've been thinking about your offer.'

'Offer?' Frank looked puzzled.

'To help sort my drains out.'

'Yes and?'

'Yes if you wouldn't mind. That would be very kind of you,' she said, hoping she'd made a sensible decision.

'Brill. We'll make the arrangements tomorrow then,' he said a big grin spreading across his face.

'Ok, So we'll see you tomorrow then?' she asked hopefully.

'Try and stop me.'

Frank paused at the door to pick up his boots, turned and blew her a kiss. 'Guten tag Schatz,' he said and left.

Liz tried to remember her schoolgirl German, but failed to recall that he had called her 'sweetheart.'

'Missing you already,' she whispered and the gloom descended again on her spirits.

Chapter 8

Afghanistan

Ahead of him the soldier was walking slowly, sweeping the vallon methodically across their route on the faint path in the sand, moving with metronomic precision, left to right, right to left, left to right.

Occasionally, a faint beep emanated from the mine detector and the team immediately stopped and took up defensive positions where they stood in single file, ten metres apart.

Vigilance increased to spot any sudden movements in the surrounding areas. Was it an ambush? Heart rates increased. Adrenaline flowed and apprehension lined their faces as the suspicious contact was meticulously revisited. The detectorist hovered the head of the vallon fractionally above the hot desert floor. Satisfied after a further examination that it was nothing to worry about, he moved on again leading the others...left to right, right to left, left to right.

William was sweating profusely as he followed behind his lead man. The weight of his bulky 150 pound armoured bomb suit gave him a strange gait as he waddled behind the mine detectorist.

The small group approached the suspected bomb. It was a fifty gallon oil drum placed outside a school.

While William and the detectorist went forward to examine the suspected bomb, the team took up defensive positions.

After carefully checking around the oil drum for any wires or trip switches the soldier with the metal detector withdrew. This time, the metronomic sweeping was slightly faster.

William was now by himself. It was all down to him alone. The world receded.

He looked into the top of the open oil drum and carefully moved a sack that covered the contents. As he moved it aside he could see a circuit board and a small collection of multi-coloured wires taped together with black insulating tape.

'Smithy,' he called to his deputy over his radio.

'Roger. Receiving you Boss.'

'I confirm it is a bomb. Tell the guys we're going to be here for a while.'

'Roger boss.'

William examined the oil drum and estimated that it contained about 10 pounds of plastic explosives. If it detonated this would set off a sympathetic explosion with the shells and grenades beneath it creating a deadly shower of hot shrapnel. He would be vaporised.

He had already made the decision not to use the robot to explode the device because of the collateral damage it would cause to the local school building nearby. Although it had been evacuated, the building was a precious commodity for the small community.

He knew that documenting the construction of the device was just as important as defusing and retrieving it to provide forensic evidence. The evidence would be used by his colleagues to disarm similar devices. But it was important for his own kudos, to tackle the intellectual challenge that the bomb maker had set him. For him, defusing the bomb was like doing the Times crossword. Difficult but satisfying.

In any case, he had a sneaking admiration for the bomb maker too. The stakes were high. One wrong move would have fatal consequences in spite of wearing the heavy protective bomb suit.

His helmet camera had already transmitted their long walk to the site of the bomb and now, by switching on his chest camera, it would record all his movements and actions whilst he gave a running commentary defusing the IED.

Immediately after, he would review all the footage and commentary when he wrote up his report … if successful. Otherwise someone else could see what had gone wrong and ensure no-one else experienced the same outcome.

He knew from failed attempts by some of his colleagues that the new bomb maker was using a booby trap wiring configuration. Consequently, if the wrong wire was cut, the device would explode.

This was his challenge as he knelt down and studied the wiring loom. First he decided to cut the tape holding the wires together so that he could trace each one. He removed one of his thick protective gloves to enable him to manipulate a scalpel to achieve the task. Slowly he went about his job. Nothing was rushed. He took his time, calmly slicing through the tape, making sure he didn't cut into the thin plastic insulation of the wires.

He possessed infinite patience, something which he knew irritated Liz.

Satisfied he'd removed the necessary tape, he gently prised open the wires and studied the resulting 'bird's nest'.

Fortunately for him the wiring block had been disturbed when the oil drum had been positioned, exposing a series of looping wires.

Methodically he traced the wires and drew a circuit diagram in his head, repeating his vision to Smithy, who was drawing it on paper as he relayed what he was seeing.

Not until he had painstakingly traced all the wiring did he stop and discuss his thoughts with him. As he did so Smithy advised him that one of his colleagues was currently on a similar job and wanted to speak to him on the air.

'Yes that's OK. We're encrypted anyway. Put him on.'

After a few seconds of clicks and bangs he heard the distorted voice of his mentor Pete.

'Hi William, [static] how [static] doing?'

'Pete...Pete can you hear me OK. Signal keeps coming and going here.'

'Yes, I [static] hear you OK.'

'This is a bit unusual. To what do I owe the honour of the call?'

'Sounds like you [static] me are dealing with the same [static]. Mine's outside an A & E department so [static] reluctant to get the robot to blast it. How far are you into [static] job?'

'Sorry Pete, your signal is very poor.'

'[static] your signal is breaking up here too.'

'Well I've got a good idea of the circuitry. OK so far?
'Yes, [static] ahead.'
'This guy is good. He's even thrown in a few redundant components to mislead me.' Ok so far?'
'Did [static] say components?'
'Redundant. I say again redundant components.'
'Yes [static] redundant. Roger. Go ahead.'
'He's used the same coloured wiring twisted together to make tracing them difficult. OK so far?'
'Colour [static] twisted'
'Yes, However, I think the booby trap fire wire is the violet one.'
'No [static] say [static].'
'Sorry Pete, lost you altogether then. I repeat the colour wire is Violet. I spell. Victor, Indigo, Oscar, Lima, Echo, Tango. Roger?'
[Static]
'Pete you receiving over?'
[Static]
Smithy's voice came on. 'Sorry boss, we appear to have lost him. He's operating from an area where there's a lot of radio interference. To add to our problems we have a large group of spectators collecting out here. The boys are feeling a bit threatened. How much longer do you think you'll be?'
'Not long I don't think. It looks like our friendly bomb maker has used a sleeve at both ends to mark the important wire.'
'What about disconnecting the battery?' Smithy suggested.
'No. I reckon if I cut the supply off to the relay, releasing it will trigger the detonator.'

[Static] You receiving [static] William? Over.'

Ah, you're back. 'Did you hear what I said Pete?'

'Yes. [static] Just about. OK. I see where you're coming from. Let me [static] check of this one.'

The communications link went silent for a few minutes and then Pete's voice came through the static.

'Yes it sounds [static] it's one and the same. So you reckon the [static] wire?'

'Go again with the colour wire.' William demanded 'I wouldn't want you cutting the wrong one. I'd never hear the last of it.'

'Too true, I'd [static] back [static] haunt you,' the other joked. 'Wire is Violet. Roger?'

'Yes, that's a roger,' William confirmed. 'Look out for the sleeved wire. Did you get that Pete? Over.'

'No I think we've lost him again.' Smithy informed him. The static in his earpiece disappeared as the comms link with Pete was cut. 'Boss the natives are getting restless.'

'OK. No time to waste. Well, here goes then,' William said, carefully positioning the cutters over the wire, his hand shaking slightly as he pushed against the resistance of his bulky protection suit.

Just as he felt the cutting edge of the cutters go through the plastic insulation of the wire, the nose of the cutters slipped.

'Shit, I've just fumbled that,' William informed Smithy.

The errant tool touched against the printed circuit board that held the components and a noise emanated from the device.

With a slight increase of his heart rate, but otherwise undaunted, he snipped the wire anyway, fully expecting to be consumed in a fireball and deafened by a loud explosion. But the noise was not the end of his life. It was instead an electronic 'woody woodpecker' laugh. The bomb maker clearly had a sense of humour and had used the ringing circuit of a mobile phone to generate the noise.

'You bastard,' William said sitting back on his haunches and smiling. 'You nearly had me there.'

'You OK Boss?' the voice in his headset asked.

'Yes. The bastard put a ringer in the circuit so I had Woody Wood pecker laughing at my cock-up when I cut the wire.'

William knelt back up and peering into the device he said. 'Well, I wonder what other surprises you've got in store for me?'

But there were no other surprises and he carefully and painstakingly dismantled the IED successfully.

'That's it Smithy. Let's make like a shepherd and get the flock out of here.' William ordered carrying the components of the IED in the evidence bag. 'I've unloaded all the nasty toys in the drum so we can get them transported back to base. Fortunately they weren't booby trapped.'

The team was in a buoyant mood as they made their way back. This was potentially the last job they would be doing before heading home for good. And they had all survived the posting intact.

However, on arriving back at the base the CO called William into the office while the team unloaded the 'booty' from their transport.

'Take a seat William.'

'Thanks Sir. I apologise for my sweaty appearance but that air conditioning in the bomb suit is next to useless and I...' William could see something in the CO's eyes that made him stop mid-sentence.

'William, I have some tragic news.'

'Sir?'

'I'm afraid that Pete wasn't as lucky as you. The IED he was defusing blew up prematurely and he died in the massive explosion that followed.'

William's heart sank. Pete was the man who had looked after him since he had been out there. He was his mentor. His buddy. They were like minded.

'Damn this god awful job,' he whispered. 'I hope the bastard who made the IED goes to hell,' he said cursing the bomb maker. 'God. Was it my fault? Perhaps he misheard me.'

'We'll have to see and hear the recordings before we can understand what went wrong. In the meantime, well done on doing a damn fine job. These people desperately want to provide education for their children and you helped today by putting your life on the line and saving the school.'

'Thank you Sir.'

William went to his tent. He lay back on his cot and stared sightlessly at the roof, his heart heavy.

Before they finally packed everything up William was keen to understand what had gone wrong with Pete's defusing of the IED.

William watched with great apprehension when he eventually reviewed the recording and commentary of Pete's fatal session. This was, after all, the death of his guru.

As the recording ran, Pete was his usual meticulous self. William winced when he heard the poor quality of the sound of their conversation together. Pete's helmet and chest cam showed the cutters clamping the violet wire with the marked sleeve and as he said 'thanks William', the screen went blank.

Pete had been blasted to smithereens.

William was devastated. He felt totally responsible. It was his advice that Pete had followed...for some inexplicable reason it had been wrong. He had effectively killed his mentor.

'Run that last bit again just before Pete cuts the wire.' William directed.

The technician did as he was bid and found the right section.

'Right pause it there. There is something different. I can't put my finger on it. Bring up my recording as well.'

William studied the two images and shook his head in frustration. 'No. I can't see it. Hang on a second. Well, there it is. The bomber has sleeved a different wire. It wasn't exactly the same as mine. God! Pete trusted in me and I let him down.'

Chapter 9

Frank arrived at Liz's flat as arranged. He had his hands full with two tool bags.

Liz was apprehensive. She had let this comparative stranger into her world. Meeting him in the pub had been alright but now it was personal.

'Hi Frank. Thanks for coming,' she greeted him lightly.

'My pleasure to see you as always,' he smoothed. 'Right. Where's the drains then?' Frank asked looking around. 'Course the trouble with these basement flats is that you've already got gravity working against you.'

'What will you do?' Liz asked, standing back.

'I've brought our sewer camera with me so let's see if we can find out any blockages that might be causing the problems. I notice you haven't got trees around here. They're usually the cause of blocked up sewers. The roots go for the water.

Frank found a manhole cover which seemed to fit into her plumbing system. He built up the sewer trolley and camera and started feeding it down one of the pipes.

'Oh. Before I go any further I need to take off my bracelet. Don't want to get that stuff on it.'

'Oh that's nice. Is it solid gold?' Liz asked, studying it.

'No, but its gold plated I think. My mother gave it to me.'

She took it off him and put it in the flat for safe keeping.

As Frank fed the trolley further into the sewer he invited Liz to watch on his little monitor screen.

'Oh, what's that?' she said, as a faint white object came into view half blocking the pipe.

'If I'm not mistaken that's probably the cause of your flooding. I think it's a terry nappy.'

'A terry nappy? Must have been down there a long time. I don't know of anybody with babies around here.'

'What you going to give me for clearing it out then?' he asked suggestively.

'A cup of tea, if you're lucky.' Liz said firmly.

'Oh is that all.' He feigned disappointment. 'OK I suppose it's better than nothing. Let's see if we can't drag it out.'

'How?' she asked.

'You're pretty slim,' he joked, 'I was going to send you down there.'

'Very funny. No, how are you going to get it out really?'

'Watch,' he instructed her.

As he did so he pressed a button on the control panel beneath the monitor screen and a small grab hand moved in to view.

He operated another switch when the 'hand' had reached the material which seized it.

Slowly he manoeuvred the trolley backwards and it started pulling the nappy away with it.

Unfortunately the material ripped as it backed out but Frank continued to retract the trolley until it was back in the mouth of the manhole, he took the ripped nappy from the grab arm and sent the trolley back down again.

Liz in the meantime took the rotten material from Frank and cagily put it into a rubbish bag.

A flood of sewage suddenly came in to the mouth of the manhole including a small armada of used condoms.

'These yours?' he asked mischievously.

'No of course not,' she said, embarrassed by the flotsam.

'Well somebody's been busy and or lucky. There must be a dozen there.'

Frank did the same exercise several times until he was satisfied he had removed the blockage. He invited Liz to kneel down beside him and check she was happy.

Liz knelt down as invited and put her hand on his shoulder to steady herself while she looked at the screen.

Her fragrance filled his nostrils overcoming the stink of the sewer.

'See, it's all gone. Hopefully that's sorted your problem out. Now about payment?' He turned, looked into Liz's eyes and moved forward as if to kiss her.

She was suddenly overcome by his closeness and in her haste to defuse the situation she stood up too quickly, which caused her to faint.

Her legs buckled underneath her and she collapsed heavily in a heap immediately next to Frank.

Initially he thought she was messing around and then he realised something serious had happened.

He was shocked and totally at a loss to know what to do. He needed help.

He looked in the car park to see if there was anyone else around to help. But there was no-one.

He was on his own and had to deal with it. He had left his mobile at home so couldn't call for an ambulance either.

Although he was not first aid trained he vaguely recalled something about the kiss of life and chest compressions but had no idea how to administer them.

So rather than waste any more time he clamped his lips over Liz's and kissed her passionately at the same time blowing into her mouth.

Panicking, he put his hand hesitantly on her chest, feeling a bit like a pervert, and started pumping her rib cage. The activity helped Liz come around.

However, as Liz became conscious she was confused and thought William was home and returned the kiss.

She opened her eyes and saw that it was Frank with whom she was engaging in a bout of tongue wrestling. She allowed the kiss to continue for a split second longer while her brain tried to work out what was going on. Then she quickly pushed him away.

'What are you doing?' she asked indignantly.

'I was saving your life,' he said, hurt at her tone. 'Giving you the kiss of life and chest compressions.'

'Saving my life! I only fainted. And get your hand off my chest,' she said, pushing his hand away. 'Anyway, you don't do the kiss of life like that.'

'I'm willing to take lessons,' he said lustfully, still tasting the sweetness of her lips. 'With you as my teacher if you like.'

'Don't be so stupid,' she replied tersely. Her look of disdain indicating he had misread her mood.

'It worked for you…and for me come to that,' he said under his breath, feeling the bulge in his trousers.

Liz was feeling light headed and had difficulty getting her bearings.

'Did you hurt anything when you fell?' Frank asked, concerned.

'No…no I don't think so,' she said, running her hand through her hair. 'I don't think I banged anything.'

'You gave me quite a shock. I thought you'd died on me. I wondered what the hell was going on. So, you sure you're OK now?' he asked, with genuine concern.

'Yes I think so,' she said, weakly.

'Can I help you to a chair?' And without waiting for an answer he scooped her up off the floor. Showing great tenderness he carried her into the flat and gently lowered her into one of the easy chairs.

She was still feeling strange and allowed him to do it.

'Right, if you're OK I'll just finish the job off.'

'Yes. Please don't worry about me. I'm OK,' she said feebly.

Frank replaced the manhole cover and quickly cleared up his tools. 'I'll just put these back in my car and if you wouldn't mind I'll wash my hands and… take payment.'

'Yeah, whatever,' Liz said vaguely. She struggled out of the chair and put the kettle on before dizzily moving on to the settee where she sat down and closed her eyes.

Frank came back in. 'Umm where's the bathroom?' he asked.

Liz pointed vaguely in the general direction. He followed her out stretched arm and soon emerged after washing his hands and arms.

'Oh before I forget, have you got my bracelet?' he asked.

'Bracelet? Oh god. Now where did I put it for safe keeping?' She wracked her brains to recollect where she'd put it.

'Oh it doesn't matter now. You're obviously not feeling well. If you find it you can give it to me in the pub sometime.

Liz struggled to get up.

'No don't trouble yourself. I'll make the tea. I'll find it. Don't worry.

While he was looking for the tea things he found the picture of Liz and William that she'd hidden before his arrival.

'Oh. So I wasn't wrong. She's playing the game while he's serving away. I knew I'd seen her wearing a wedding ring. Looks like my luck's in.' Frank thought, remembering the softness of her kiss.

Chapter 10

The following day whilst Liz was getting ready for work she was horrified to hear on the radio news that a Bomb Disposal officer had been killed whilst defusing an IED in Afghanistan.

She immediately called the 'emergency only' number that William had given her.

After what seemed an eternity the call was answered.

'Hello.'

'William! William is that you?'

'Yes.'

'Oh thank god! Are you alright? I've just heard on the news about a soldier being killed. As I hadn't heard from you, I assumed the worst. After I heard that a Bomb Disposal man had been…'

'Explosive Ordnance Disposal…' he corrected.

'Yeah whatever,' she continued, ignoring his pedantic correction,'…had been killed. I'm so glad to hear your voice. Are you sure you're OK?'

'Yes,' William replied, monosyllabically.

'Was he one of your team?' she asked cautiously.

'It was Pete,' he said flatly.

'Oh no!' she said, shocked. 'Not Pete.'

'It was my fault.' William blurted.

'What do you mean it was your fault?' Were you with him?'

'As good as. I told him which wire to cut and…'
'When? How?' she stuttered.
'It happened the other day. I can't remember when.'
'But they've only just announced it,' she informed him.
'It's always delayed announcing it to the press.'
'Oh William, I'm so sorry. But you've always said he was so meticulous. He never trusted anybody but himself.'
'Except me…and I let him down. He's dead Liz. Dead! I killed him,' he sobbed.

She listened to his pitiful sobbing frustrated by the three thousand miles that separated them and feeling totally helpless at being unable to cradle him or console him. After a few minutes he stopped crying and said, 'I'll call you back.'
'When are you coming home?'
'Don't know. Soon, I think.'
Suddenly he hung up.
She sat down and stared at the phone. Relief that finding he was OK and then the enormity of Pete's death hit her hard. The tears came in torrents.
'Oh God. Poor William. Poor William,' she sobbed, the knot of anguish tight in her stomach.

Chapter 11

The party was in full swing when Frank arrived back at the rugby club. He could hear the booming music even before he could see the building.

Although he had showered immediately after the game and had a couple of pints in the club house to celebrate the 14 – 7 win, he had gone to his digs and relaxed in a foam filled bath to ease his aches and pains.

It had been a hard, but successful game and he'd come away sporting a black eye from someone's errant elbow. Pumped up on adrenalin during the game the endorphins had stopped the eye from hurting until he was relaxing in the bath.

He was pleased with himself. He had scored another try to add to his season total of four. He enjoyed the game. His number 14 position on the right wing was ideal for his fast pace and wiry agility to dodge tackles.

Always a popular member of the team, his mates cheered his arrival back at the club. In recognition of his contribution to scoring the winning try the team captain insisted on buying him a pint.

The volume of the disco made talking difficult. Frank quickly ended up with 'disco throat' after attempting to hold a conversation with them.

Many of his team mates were glued to each other's ears shouting to make themselves heard too. No wonder there were so many people outside with their drinks,' he thought.

The room was uncomfortably hot from the sheer volume of people in the small club house. Many of whom had retired to their tables which surrounded the small dance floor and were content just to watch the dancers. Conversations were difficult and drinks were re-ordered by gesticulations and thumbs up signs to each other.

Bathed in the pulsating multicolour light from the disco, he could see a lot of women gyrating to the music. But few men.

Pint in hand, he wandered over to look at the twirling group to suss out any new 'talent' amongst them.

He had downed half of his drink when he saw her. Liz was dancing with a girlfriend in the middle of the dance floor.

'Ah ha,' he thought, 'I wonder who she's with?'

The DJ's voice broke into the music. He said something incomprehensible and changed the CD to a slower number. Obviously he misread his audience as many left the dance floor and headed back to their tables to re-hydrate.

Frank watched Liz make her way to a table and was relieved to see there were no men sitting there.

'Might be in with a chance here,' he thought making his way to an empty chair by the side of her. As he did so he was treated to the waft of her perfume. The heavenly aroma made his pulses race. She was looking at the dancers and didn't see him arrive.

'Is it hot in here, or is it just you that's hot?' he shouted in her ear.

'Oh you made me jump …,' she said in surprise, putting her hand over her heart. She stopped in mid-sentence when she saw who it was. 'Oh, I might have guessed it was you with that pathetic chat up line,' she shouted, smiling.

He shook his head as if he hadn't heard what she said and put his ear to her lips in order for her to repeat it. He was enjoying the close proximity of them again.

After a few abortive attempts, they stopped trying to talk to each other and waited for a quiet moment.

They didn't have to wait too long as the DJ's over modulated voice announced something about food being available and at the same time he put on a quieter CD. He made a beeline himself to the buffet table and headed up the queue.

'Thank Christ for that,' Frank said, without having to shout. 'I think all these bleedin' DJs are deaf with the volume that high, when all everybody wants to do really is have a beer and a chat.'

'You sound like a grumpy old man,' she said. 'You need to 'feel' the music to dance.'

'Perhaps you'll show me later on after you've given me lessons on the Kiss of Life. By the way how is your plumbing now?

Liz blushed at the mention of the plumbing incident. In spite of feeling queasy from fainting she had enjoyed his version of the kiss of life. And his attempt at chest compressions.

'Yes. The drains are OK thanks. I'm sorry I'm not qualified to give first aid training.' she added awkwardly.

'Pity I'm a quick learner. But practice makes perfect,' he smirked.

Someone put the main lights on so that people could see the contents of the buffet table.

Immediately the revellers started leaving their tables and headed for the refreshments. The club caterers had been busy preparing a mountain of food. The table was groaning under the weight of it. Sausage and filled rolls, fresh tiger bloom bread and cheese, crisps, pork pie slices, salad and sliced beetroot enticed the revellers.

'Can I buy you a drink?' he asked hopefully.

'Yes, you can,' she slurred. 'But you'll have to buy my friend one as well because it's my round.'

Her friend had finished the conversation with the person next to her and turned around to speak to Liz then noticed Frank. 'Aren't you going to introduce me to your charming companion?' she asked, studying Frank.

'Mel, this is...oh dear I've forgotten your name,' she lied.

'Well, I obviously made a lasting impression on you,' he said. 'Frank. Frank you, frank you very much,' he said delivering a poor Tommy Cooper impression.

'Frank. Pleased to meet you,' Mel said, proffering her hand. 'I'm Melanie.'

Frank kissed the back of her hand,' Charmed I'm sure. Pleased to meet you too Melanie.'

'Watch him Mel. He's a smooth talker.' Liz added.

Liz then spotted his damaged eye. 'I see somebody made an impression on you too.'

'What do you mean?' he said puzzled, having forgotten about his damaged eye.

'Your eye,' she said studying it closely. 'Have you been fighting?'

'Yes I fought off several guys to get to sit next to you,' he smoozed

'See what I mean Mel. Full of bull,' Liz said, laughing.

'No. This is my trophy for scoring the winning try today.' Frank proudly announced.

'Oh you play rugby?' Mel said unnecessarily.

'Amongst other games,' he said and seductively rubbed shoulders with Liz.

'Anyway. About this drink.' Liz quickly changed the subject. 'Rum and Coke for me and a red wine for you Mel?'

'Yes please.'

'I know when I'm defeated,' he said, going to the bar.

'Oh my God. Where did you find him Liz? He's absolutely gorgeous.' Mel oozed.

'I didn't. He found me.' Liz filled Mel in with the encounter in the Flying Machine. 'And he sorted out my plumbing too.'

'What sort of plumbing?' Mel asked suspiciously.

'I had a flood in my basement.'

'Oh that sort of plumbing, I thought you meant... you know.'

'You've got a dirty mind missy.' Liz scolded.

'So you and him?' Mel asked suspiciously.

'Of course not. He's only a kid.' Liz said, trying to sound casually disinterested to hide her smouldering interest in him.

'I reckon he's got to be mid to late twenties.' Mel said surveying the young rugby player. 'So you're not that much older.'

'If you call ten years my junior not being that much older,' she argued unconvincingly.

'Yes. But what a catch,' Mel continued. 'If you're not interested, move aside and let me have a go,' she said ogling Frank at the bar.

'Beside which, you're forgetting. I'm married.' Liz said, without much conviction. For although she was concerned about William's state of mind following Pete's death, she couldn't do anything about it while he was away and decided to have a good time at the dance.

'Yes, but for how much longer? Let's face it Liz, you haven't been happy for a long time, have you?'

'William and I are OK,' Liz added unconvincingly.

Frank bumped into the team captain at the bar. 'Sorry skipper. Didn't see you there. How's it going?'

'I'm OK. Looks like you are too. You know she's married, don't you? '

'Yeah I know. But how do you?'

'Her old man's in the army. I've been on tour with him.'

'What a rugby tour?'

'No. I'm in the TA. I've done a tour in Afghanistan with his regiment.'

'Yeah, but you can't blame me for trying can you? I reckon she's up for it. She's even taken her wedding ring off. She thinks I hadn't spotted it.'

'I wouldn't mess with an army man's wife,' the captain counselled.

'Why's that?'

'They're trained killers,' the rugby captain said dramatically. 'And they got a lot of mates who don't take kindly to people poaching their women either.'

'Come on. I can't turn this gift horse down. She's serving it to me on a plate.'

'She's an officer's wife.'

'So will it be pistols at dawn then?' Frank joked. 'Anyway I quite like her.'

'What happened to your last one? Who was it now?'

'Chelsea.'

'Yeah. So what happened to her?'

'I'm avoiding single Mothers from now on. They're too clingy and maternal. No, I quite fancy Liz. She's a bit of fun.'

'OK. But I bet you don't get past first base with her.'

'You're on. With my charms, she's as good as another notch on my head board already. Anyway I ain't got time to chat to you. I've got hunting to do. See you.'

Frank arrived back at the table carrying all the drinks in his big hands.

'You going to join me at the food table ladies before it's all gone?'

They followed him to the table and moved in front of him at his invitation.

'Thank you kind Sir,' Mel said, and brushed past him seductively.

Liz and Mel selected a few crisps, sausages and a bit of salad which just about covered the bottom of their paper plates and made their way back to the table, leaving Frank loading a plate with a mountain of food.

'Need to keep my energy up, he said, re-joining them, 'Got some partying to do tonight with you two ladies.' And he duly tucked into his large banquet.

When the disco resumed Frank danced with both of them but made sure he ended the night dancing closely with Liz...getting up close and personal in a smooch.

'Did I hear somebody say that you're married?' Frank queried.

'Maybe,' Liz answered, wrong footed by the question.

'But I didn't hear them say, happily.' Frank smiled and wrapped his arms around her in a smothering embrace.

Liz moulded into him and returned his advances, drunk with a euphoric feeling that she had not experienced for many years in her dormant marriage.

At the end of the evening Mel, having conceded defeat in the passion stakes, nevertheless decided she needed to rescue Liz from wrecking her marriage. She duly grabbed her arm and dragged her away from Frank. The pair reluctantly unpeeled from each other but not before they kissed.

'Come on you two. Get your tongue out of her throat Frank.' Mel said and steered a reluctant Liz to the door.

As they were departing Frank shouted, 'hey, haven't you forgotten something?'

The girls checked each other for any missing items and looked at him blankly.

'No,' they chorused.

'What about me?' Frank said hopefully.

Mel giggled and pushed an unwilling and slightly drunk Liz out of the club.

'See you soon Liz,' Frank called as the girls disappeared into the night.

'I hope so,' Liz thought. 'I really hope so,' her heart beating wildly.

CHAPTER 12

During the night of the dance Frank had managed to get Liz's mobile number from Mel by persuading her he had forgotten the number Liz had previously given him.

'I need it so that I can make arrangements to do some plumbing work for her,' he lied.

Mel was not convinced.' Why don't you ask her yourself then?'

'I don't want to embarrass myself admitting I'd forgotten it,' he suggested weakly.

With a knowing smile Mel gave him the number. 'Be careful what you're up to. Remember she's a married woman.'

'What are you suggesting? It's only to do with her pipes. That's all.'

'Yes I can imagine. But which ones?'

So having now gained the number, Frank sent her a text message.

'I found UR nbr in the angel's directory. Now U have mine 2.'

Liz looked at the message. She didn't recognise the number and wondered who'd sent it. She decided to ignore it initially, but her curiosity got the better of her and she replied.

'Who RU?'

The reply came almost immediately. '*I haven't been able to find my heart since the dance, I think you must have stolen it.*'

'Oh Frank, you're so full of BS even on your mobile,' she laughed.

Quickly she replied, '*Not guilty, your honour.*'

'*Look fwd 2 Cing U at the pub 2 do a full body search 2 make sure.*'

'*In your dreams Rugby boy.*'

'*Yes, that's right. I dream of U constantly. U R my dream girl.*'

Liz was flattered by his attention and enjoyed dreaming about the fantasy of an illicit love affair, in spite of her moral standards about no hanky panky during tour absences. She had seen many marriages founder as a result. However, her firm resolve was weakening. 'William obviously wasn't interested in her to even let her know he was safe,' she thought.

But she didn't think there was any harm in responding to some of Frank's less outrageous texts.

Chapter 13

It had been a week since Pete died in the massive explosion. William was lying fully dressed on his cot staring at the roof of the tent. His eyes focussed on nothing, his packed camouflaged rucksack standing nearby.

He made no effort to move at the sound of approaching footsteps.

'Boss, the Chinook is here,' his deputy informed him. 'It's time to make like a shepherd and get the flock out of here.'

'Hasn't come soon enough for poor Pete though has it?' William said thickly, without moving. 'End of operations in Afghanistan. What have we achieved? Eff all.'

'Come on Boss. We came to do a job and we've done it.'

'Yeah, but not very well. Do you know that about 80% of our casualties are as a result of bombs and IEDs?'

'You said that you can't boil the ocean.' Smithy reminded him. 'One job at a time isn't that what you used to say?'

'You know there will be hundreds of them left,' William reflected pessimistically. 'We don't stand a chance of stopping it. This type of guerrilla warfare has been going on for thousands of years.'

'Yeah, I guess the IED problem has gone off the scale…it's easy killing for them. No fire fight. Just a remote detonation and bang. Another one hits the dust,' Smithy reflected.

'They don't even have to kill. Maiming is more disruptive' William added.

Yeah, but there'd be more if we hadn't done our job,' Smithy repeated. 'Anyway, you always said we needed to be in control, otherwise…

'In control! Huh! That's right. I have never felt so out of control as I do now.' William admitted.

Smithy struggled to think of something encouraging to bolster up William's flagging spirits and finally said, 'I guess it only takes one trigger situation and years of staying in control can easily disappear,' he said sympathetically.

'Yeah, just like a house of cards,' William said, closing his eyes. 'Your belief system starts disappearing and you lose control.'

'Well it's over now Boss and we've got a helicopter waiting for us.'

William ignored the reminder about leaving and carried on dolefully. 'But the danger is, you are so focussed on doing the one job, that sometimes you don't see the bigger picture.'

'Not our problem you used to tell me,' Smithy reminded him. 'We're cogs within wheels you reckoned.'

'No you're right. I suppose that's where the Generals and strategists sit isn't it? One mine, one IED is nothing to them.'

'You got to admit though Boss, it's a great crack when we defuse an IED, isn't it?'

'I used to have this romantic idea of saving communities by pitting our wits and risking our lives against an unseen enemy. But Pete's death has brought me back to earth. It's a shit job.'

'But somebody's got to do it. To defeat the people who lay these IEDs.'

'No, they're only the 'cannon fodder'.' William added. 'The insurgents don't risk losing a bomb maker to deploy their handiwork. No, the people who site them are expendable.'

'Boss the heli...'

But William wasn't listening. 'The bomb makers are the intelligent people. Some only in their teens. Geeky' computer boffins. As I know only too well. Underestimate their intelligence at your peril.'

'Tell me about it,' Smithy said, as he visualised the Memorial wall at Bastian thinking about his own fallen colleagues.

'This was mine and Pete's last job before going home,' William said quietly. 'Well, I suppose nothing's changed. Except Pete won't be walking off the plane at Brize Norton.'

'Sorry about Pete boss. I know he was your good friend.' Smithy added softly.

'He was more than a friend, Pete. He was my guru. We trusted each other implicitly. I trusted him with my life when we were in some dodgy situations and he trusted me... If you haven't got trust you have nothing.' Williams voice cracked, 'I let him down... I lost him his life.'

'No Boss, you're being too hard on yourself. The bomb maker tricked us...Pete cut the wrong wire.'

'Yes, we all know he cut the wrong friggin wire. His body is scattered all over Helmand to prove it.'

'No, what I'm saying is, you shouldn't beat yourself up about his...the explosion. He couldn't hear you very well and he didn't cut the correct wire. It's not your fault.'

'Great. So I blame the Comms team do I?'

'No, boss, I was just...it doesn't matter.' Smithy concluded, realising William was too traumatised to listen to a rational argument.

'No you're right. It doesn't matter,. He's dead is all that matters. I let him down in the worst possible way. I betrayed his trust.'

The soldier waited in deafening silence wondering what to say to the man they called the 'Iceman'.

This man was normally ice cool even in the worst situations, especially under fire when all around them were panicking. Here was the man he himself trusted with his life.

William's calm and professional approach gave him a confidence he had never felt from others. Being William's number two, Smithy had been in deadly danger almost every single day.

William's 'long walk' to confront another IED was text book. His courage walking into danger was boundless. It was as if he had a shield of invincibility surrounding him.

To see him in this distressed state was hard to stomach.

After a respectable pause he finally worked up courage to speak again.

'They're waiting for us Boss,' he said quietly. 'Do you want me to grab your rucker?'

'I'm not a frigging invalid. No I'll take it myself. Now eff off before I...'

William swung his legs off his cot, stood up and grabbed some nearby ornaments off a shelf. He looked at them for a second then threw them angrily on to the floor, smashing them to smithereens.

The iceman had totally lost it.

Smithy fidgeted before retreating out of the tent, embarrassed at seeing his officer in an angry frenzy and desperately wondering what to do.

Chapter 14

Liz drove to Brize Norton to pick William up from the military airport. After passing through several security checks she eventually entered the arrivals lounge. She held small and meaningless conversations with other service wives, some of whom she had met before, others she only vaguely remembered. Being off the camp and away from married quarters she had become detached from the social side of being an officer's wife.

Liz's heart was in her mouth as the Airbus A330 Voyager touched down. A puff of smoke announced its landing as the wheels kissed the runway. While the plane was on the taxiway a large C17 Globemaster transport plane also touched down.

The taxiing aircraft seemed to take an age to manoeuvre around the airfield before finally heading towards the terminal buildings. It was another frustratingly long period before the steps were positioned for the passengers to alight.

Then, at last, the passenger door of the Voyager opened and the excitement amongst the waiting families became an audible chatter.

A chameleon of soldiers still dressed in their desert camouflage uniforms started exiting the plane and descending the steps.

Liz searched expectantly for William, but couldn't see him in the euphoric waving line of smiling faces.

Suddenly the doors of the arrivals lounge were opened and a small stampede of relatives avalanched on to the edge of the airfield where a line of traffic cones had been placed to indicate their border.

Excited children, oblivious to the regulations, ran excitedly towards the approaching line of servicemen and women.

A chorus of 'Daddy...daddy'; 'Mummy...mummy' rose from the rushing children.

In spite of the heavy rucksacks, uniformed arms swept their offspring up, faces covered in kisses and tears of joy. Smiles erupted as child laden soldiers searched out their partners and spouses.

Joyful scenes enfolded over the apron. Hugs, embraces and long passionate kisses that promised more later.

Liz stood among the excited crowd and was getting anxious that William didn't appear to be with them. Then she spotted him twenty metres from the back of the line of euphoric soldiers. Head down. A lonely figure.

Because of his guilt over Pete's death she knew his homecoming was not going to be the joyful event that everyone else was experiencing.

Meanwhile, the enormous Globemaster had also come to a halt and the huge ramp at the back of the plane had been lowered. An attendant army was waiting. Within a few moments they were efficiently attending to the various loads of equipment held in its vast bowels.

Three black hearses drove towards the stationary plane and parked nearby. An honour guard of smartly uniformed soldiers was formed in front of them.

Above the excitement of the family reunions Liz could see three separate groups of soldiers marching smartly up to the ramp of the C17. These were the men chosen to carry the precious cargo, the coffins of their fallen colleagues who were being repatriated. Amongst them would be Pete.

The flood of joyful soldiers, partners and offspring passed Liz in a babble of excitement heading into the airport lounge.

She looked at William's sad face and decided she couldn't wait any longer. She ran to him, put her arms around his neck and embraced him tightly.

She wanted to say 'William I'm overjoyed to see you.' But his glum face suggested otherwise. Instead she said 'I'm so sorry William,' and tightened her embrace.

William dropped his rucksack and finally returned the embrace, enfolding her in his strong arms. She could feel his body shaking as he sobbed on her shoulder trying to hide his tears.

'It'll be alright,' she whispered, stroking his hair.

'It was my fault. Pete's dead,' he sobbed.

Liz was shocked by his outpouring of grief. Normally William rarely showed his feelings.

'No, you mustn't blame yourself,' she soothed. 'Shit happens. Isn't that what you're always telling me?'

'I gave him bad advice and he died.' William wept.

'Come on William, let's go home,' Liz said softly, stepping away from him and taking his hand.

'No. I must stay and pay my respects to Pete and the other two,' he said visibly getting himself together and standing to attention facing the plane. Others re-emerged from the airport terminal and formed a silent line.

At that moment the first group of six soldiers emerged from the belly of the C17, on their shoulders a Union Jack covered coffin. In perfect step they carefully marched down the ramp. At the front a sergeant walked backwards, firmly pushing against the front of the casket to prevent it sliding off the bearers shoulders. Behind the first group came two other groups of smartly uniformed soldiers carrying coffins similarly bedecked in a Union flag.

The three groups slowly marched towards the line of waiting hearses.

'That should have been me,' William said quietly.

'I'm glad it wasn't,' Liz said squeezing his hand tightly.

They followed the cortege to the Memorial Garden at Norton Way to allow William to pay his respects in front of the flag pole upon which the Union Flag from Royal Wootton Bassett was flying.

Smithy joined him briefly before heading home with wife.

'Take care Boss. Hope you feel better soon. Don't forget. If you need anything. Just bell me.'

Finally Liz drove them home.

William's sombre mood created a heavy atmosphere which Liz could not bring herself to break with small talk.

William stared forward through unseeing eyes, the thousand yard stare suffered by many service people who experience combat trauma.

Liz decided now wasn't the time to remind him of his anniversary omission. But it was an angry bird caged in her head that needed to be released- sometime.

Chapter 15

They arrived back in Cheltenham after a silent journey. The atmosphere in the car had remained tense. Liz was desperate to talk to William about a million things but she judged now wasn't the right time.

William was beside her in body only. His mind was wrapped in despair thousands of miles away.

They unloaded the car and descended down the worn steps into the basement flat.

'Well, home at last,' Liz said, trying to sound bright, but feeling depressed that William had returned in such a sad state.

She had been excited about his return, especially as there was going to be no more tours of Afghanistan. But now she wasn't so sure. He was creating an energy sapping atmosphere. A blanket of gloom had descended over the place and her excitement had been strangled.

'Cuppa?' she asked desperate to break the silence.

'No, I'll have a shower and catch up with some shuteye,' he said gloomily, dumping his luggage on the lounge floor.

Liz tutted at the violation of the room she had spent hours cleaning. Nevertheless, she bottled her frustration of his thoughtless invasion to her ordered space.

'I've put your stuff in the bathroom,' she said, filling the kettle.

Normally on his return from 'operations' they would shower together. It was the start of their rekindled passion. But not today she decided. Now was not the time while he was wallowing in his own misery.

As he was making his way into the bathroom William spotted the anniversary cards from their best man and chief bridesmaid perched on the mantelpiece of the boarded off fireplace.

'Oh, shit, I know there was something I was going to do. I'm sorry I...things just got in the way,' William confessed. 'I had it on my to-do list but what with a raid on a bomb factory, an urgent IED and poor Pete, it got forgotten. I'm sorry, I'll make it up to you,' he proposed.

'I should think so too.' The angry bird had made an escape. Liz could no longer contain her anger. She couldn't stop her outburst. 'You come home here with a face like thunder and full of self-pity. What about me? I was worried to death when I heard the news about the explosion and the death of an EOD man. I had to call you to make sure you were alright. It wouldn't have hurt you to have called me would it? But not you. Oh no! You were just thinking of yourself,' she rattled on angrily.

'What? I can't believe how pathetic you sound. Wittering on about a bleeding missing anniversary card,' William said, flabbergasted. 'Pete is dead. Don't you understand that? He was blown to smithereens. Do you understand?' he shouted in her face.

'Yes of course I do and I'm sorry.'

'It wasn't because he had forgotten to send a bloody card. Somebody wanted him dead and I helped them succeed.'

Liz needed to vent her frustration but her anger overcame her sensibility 'Well we all have our crosses to bear,' she replied angrily and instantly regretted it.

At that moment William lost his self-control and slapped her across the face. They were both horrified. He had never been violent to her during their long association.

She put her hand up to her smarting cheek and holding back the tears she yelled angrily, 'don't you ever do that again.'

He looked at his hand in horror as if it had acted by itself. He wanted to disown it's actions.

He dissolved into tears, 'I'm sorry, I'm sorry,' he sobbed. 'I...I didn't mean to, I didn't mean to. It won't happen again I promise.'

'You're dead right there,' she screamed, feeling the redness of his handprint spreading across her cheek. 'You ever dare touch me again and I shall leave you.'

'I'm so...sorry ...I don't know what I'll do if you left me...I need you so much.'

He dropped to his knees and covered his face with his big hands and cried, his body wracked with grief.

'Don't you know what it's like for me ...waiting to hear if you're safe? I've got a life too.' Liz filled up as well.

'But Pete doesn't anymore,' he sobbed.

She moved towards him, her anger now neutralised by his breakdown. She put her hands gently on his head, spread her fingers through his hair, feeling his hot scalp.

He lifted his head, thrusting his tear streaked face into her stomach. His strong arms encircled her small waist. Holding tightly he continued to sob.

Pity replaced her anger. 'Ssssh,' she whispered, 'Ssssh. It'll be alright, it'll be alright.' A teardrop snaked down her cheek.

She moved her long fingers though his hair to his neck, felt the sweat drenched collar and stroked his ears, all the time talking quietly, consoling him.

'It'll be alright. Don't worry. Soon it won't hurt so much. Time is a healer. Ssssh.'

Eventually his sobbing stopped. She cupped his chin and lifted his face from her now wet dress.

His eyes were bloodshot and puffy. The veins of his forehead stood out on his red sweaty face. She smoothed his hair which had stuck to his hot forehead.

'I'm so sorry, but I can't get my mind off it. Pete, the Taliban, the next bomb, the next bobby trap. '...I've had it. My nerves are shot...I've lost it...I can't do this anymore.' William blurted.

'Ssssh. Those horrors are behind you now,' she counselled gently.

'You know I love you so much,' he said dolefully. 'I need you now more than ever.'

His eyes filled again. He pulled away from her, stood up and aimlessly went to the front door. Suddenly he balled his fist and punched the centre panel of the door.

'I've had it. I'm no good for anything anymore. Look at these hands. I just can't stop them from shaking. I'm useless like this.'

'It will pass. You'll see. This is what you've always wanted to do. Remember? You are good at it.' Liz encouraged. 'You've worked so hard to achieve it'

'Maybe I was just too ambitious. Perhaps I'm not really cut out for this. Maybe I'm just...just too sensitive,' he said irrationally.

'Look at all your successes! Think of all the lives you've saved. All the injuries you've prevented.'

'I don't know any more,'

'If for no other reason, you have to do it for Pete.'

'Pete must be up there laughing at me for being so pathetic.'

'I think you're being too harsh on yourself. Nobody can go through the trauma of knowing your best mate…'

'Go on say it…blasted to a million pieces. Do you know they couldn't even find his eyes, his face, his heart, his soul. Jesus Christ. It's awful. How can you get over that?

'I think you're asking the wrong one that question,' Liz said, sitting down. 'Perhaps you can start to understand how I feel every time you go out on a job. Never knowing whether I'll see you again…waiting for the phone call to tell me you're dead. Do you know I switch the television and radio off until you call me. Only then can I relax when I know you're safe. So don't ask me about the anguish. It's because I love you that I'm still here.'

But he wasn't listening. He was wrapped up in a flashback of exploding bombs, screams of injured soldiers, the dust, the stifling heat.

'He was spread all around the debris of the effing buildings you know,' he said, wide eyed. 'Do you know they had to calculate how many bricks they had to put in his coffin to pretend he was in there.'

'Oh god how terrible,' Liz whispered, chewing her lip.

'He always said that he hadn't done enough in the Regiment to leave a mark…well he certainly left a mark out there in that place…a big red one.'

'William! That's a terrible thing to say.' Liz admonished him for his black humour. But William was still lost in his memories.

'Nobody deserves to die like that. He was trying to help the community and this is how they pay him,' he said, pacing backwards and forwards, his eyes distant. 'What was it all for?'

He suddenly stopped and gazed wide eyed at Liz expecting an answer. She shrugged her shoulders but said nothing.

William continued his rhetoric about Pete's fatal incident. 'After the dust from the explosion had settled, I gather people just carried on their daily life as if nothing had happened. The man was dead and they didn't care that he was trying to help their community.'

'I guess they're used to that sort of violence and life goes on regardless,' Liz said quietly, finding her voice.

'Except for Pete,' William ranted. 'Nobody cared about the sacrifice he made.' Huh sacrifice!' he raged. 'The politicians say the word, but they don't really know what sacrifice means...it's merely a hollow meaningless phrase said to appease the population about the death of my comrades.'

Liz had never seen William so animated before and listened surprised by his vitriol.

'The thing that hurts so much...'William struggled with the words, 'was I told him which wire to cut. It... it should have been me that died that day. Not him. Oh God, I can't do this anymore,' William said mournfully.

'William, you can't blame yourself for somebody else's mistake. Pete knew what he was doing...and his luck ran out.'

'You're not listening to me…why don't you listen? I'm talking about killing my friend. My best pal. My guilt.'

William shook his head as if disputing Liz's argument. He turned and started going into the bedroom. Liz knew she was on a losing battle and said, 'If you're going to go to bed after your shower I'll go for a run so that I don't disturb you.'

She thought about the celebrations she had planned for his homecoming which included a 'show' in Stratford upon Avon; A romantic meal at their favourite restaurant and a night of passion…but now she thought that in his state it would be a waste of time and she would cancel it all.

Chapter 16

William undressed, leaving a trail of his clothes over the flat and went into the shower.

Liz, irritated by his clutter, scooped them up, took them into the bedroom and dumped them in the dirty washing basket. She could hear the water running in the bathroom but no sound of him washing. She listened for a few minutes and concerned she called,

'Are you OK William?'

No reply.

'William!'

She left the bedroom and opened the bathroom door but almost immediately it hit something and wouldn't fully open.

'William are you OK?' she said in a panic, wondering if he'd collapsed against the door. 'Let me in sweetheart.' She pushed the door again and it moved slightly. The gap was just wide enough for her to put her head around the door. William was naked standing with his back to the door, motionless.

'Come on darling let me in.'

He moved slightly and she pushed her way in.

'You'll feel better when you've had a shower and a few hours' sleep. Let me help you.'

'No, I'm alright,' he said, sounding haunted. 'It's the flashbacks. It's difficult to get my head around this...

this tranquillity, after living in a hell hole for the last six months, always expecting an attack or a 'shout'. We had to be alert.'

William stepped into the bath and swung the glass panel into place. The spray bounced off his firm suntanned body immediately showering the gleaming glass which Liz had polished.

She so much wanted to join him in their usual ritual but resisted the temptation and left him vigorously shampooing his hair.

She changed into her running kit and waited until William had finished showering. After twenty minutes he emerged with a towel around his waist.

'Feel better for that?' she asked smiling.

'No, I've got a fearful headache. Got any pills?' he asked, holding his forehead.

'Yes, paracetamol OK?'

'Yeah, whatever.'

Liz rummaged through her handbag and found the box. She squeezed two tablets out of the blister pack and gave them to him.

'I'll get you a glass of water,' she said, going into the kitchen.

Meanwhile William made his way into the bedroom and put on a pair of pyjamas she had laid out on the bed for him.

'Here you are,' she said, giving him the glass of water. 'Do you want me for anything else?' she added, hoping his carnal desire had been aroused by his shower and he would sweep her into bed.

'No I'll try to get some sleep.'

'Hope you feel better,' she said and kissed him on the forehead. She gazed at him momentarily before closing the bedroom door quietly behind her.

'Me too,' he muttered to himself, turning on to his side. 'Let's hope the nightmares let me.'

Before she left she hid the packet of paracetamol. She didn't want his suicide on her conscience.

Chapter 17

As she started her run, the tension of the day suddenly overwhelmed her. The amalgam of her emotions reached 'critical mass' and she started crying.

Running with misty eyes she felt frustrated that she couldn't do anything to help him. She hadn't been prepared for the dramatic change in his personality. Then there was the totally out of character slap across the face. Was this a sign of worse things to come?

She recalled the days on camp when domestic violence was happening but not talked about. It was a ridiculous code of silence that helped to perpetuate the abuse.

'We all knew about the abused women,' she reflected. 'We all knew what was going on when they stopped their usual routine and stayed at home. It was generally a sign of them waiting for the bruises to disappear.' She recalled. 'They were then caught between a rock and a hard place. If they told anyone about the assault, he could be court marshalled and kicked out the army and they would probably end up homeless. Then she would have an even more abusive husband on her hands. It was a terrible dilemma, either getting beaten with a roof over your head or ending up on the streets. Life wasn't fair.

Subconsciously she followed her usual route. She wasn't taking in the views today. Just a plod.

'And of course there's the honour of the Regiment which could be besmirched if it leaked out. Therefore it must be protected at all costs,' she thought disrespectfully. 'Christ it stinks. Everybody knows it goes on and nobody does anything to stop it.'

She passed the hospital buildings without registering where she was.

At least the angst of not knowing whether he had been killed whilst abroad was now gone. But his depression had really overshadowed the forgotten anniversary card.

She put her hand up to her cheek where he'd hit her. It smarted. 'I must remember to put some blusher on to hide it,' she thought.

Liz remembered the anniversary card that she'd bought for him. A tear ran down her face and splashed on to her running top.

'I must remember to give him the card when I get back,' she thought.'

When she returned home William was up and sitting in a chair.

'Oh I didn't expect you up yet. You've barely had an hour. Do you feel better?'

'No, not really,' he grunted.

'Oh well, in that case I might as well go in to work. Oh by the way, here's your anniversary card,' she said taking it from the cupboard drawer. 'Happy belated anniversary,' she said and placed a kiss on his forehead.

Oh do you have to go? I thought we could…' He couldn't find the right words. 'No you're probably right.'

'Sorry William, I don't see the point with you in this mood. Anyway I promised the Landlord if I could, although it's not my usual rota, I would cover the bar for him…ironically it's his wedding anniversary and they're going out for a lunchtime meal. It's the only time they can leave the pub.'

She filled up at the thought of her own disastrous anniversary and abortive plans for William's homecoming. She rushed past him in to the bathroom to shower.

She showered quickly, donned her usual black polo shirt and slacks and went back into the lounge. William was still sitting where she'd left him. She went over to kiss him. He grabbed her wrist and looked into her face.

'Please don't go,' he pleaded.

'I'm sorry William, but I promised. 'I'll be back about 3:30. Why don't you try to get some sleep. I'm sure you'll feel a lot better,' she said kissing him on the cheek. He let go of her wrist and she went out through the front door leaving him gazing at the envelope in his hands.

William desperately wanted her to stay but didn't have the energy to persuade her otherwise. Slapping her had soured their relationship. This drove him even deeper in to despair. The blackness filled his mind. Where would it end?

Liz went to the pub and was greeted by a delighted Landlord who was standing by the bar.

'Oh thank you Liz for coming in on your day off, especially as I gather William is home from Afghanistan. I owe you.'

'That's OK George, I know how important it is to celebrate these anniversaries,' she said. The irony of her words did not escape her.

Is that a mark on your face?' he asked, looking at her cheek.

'Oh that, it's from when I went running earlier. I ran into a bush,' she mumbled. I put some extra blusher on it that's all.' She screamed inside. This was exactly what the army wives did, made excuses for the abuse.

The Landlord and his wife duly departed for their meal delighted that she had turned up.

Chapter 18

It had been a week since William's return home and he was slowly improving, but not fast enough for Liz's liking.

She had continued going to work in spite of William's insistence that she stayed home with him, but she felt so depressed being around him and needed to get out.

But today Liz had a dental appointment and was consequently late getting into work. George had been understanding and had covered the bar in the meantime.

Frank was already sitting at the bar and was looking mournful when Liz arrived.

'Thank goodness for that. For one moment there I thought I'd upset you and you weren't going to speak to me,' he said beaming.

'No, I had a dental appointment. Usual?' she asked spotting his near empty glass. She was already feeling happier in his presence.

'Aren't you going to give me a birthday kiss?' Frank asked as Liz handed him his pint.

'Oh is it your birthday today?'

'Yes, 21 again,' he lied.

'Yeah right!' Liz said sceptically. 'Well congratulations. If I'd known I'd have bought you a card.'

'It's a bummer having to work on my birthday though,' Frank complained.

Liz leant over the bar and intended giving him a quick peck on the cheek but Frank had other ideas. He moved just as she was pursing up and put his arm around her neck and gave her a full mouth kiss, which she didn't resist too much. Finally she pulled back and he let her go.

'Well, happy birthday,' she gasped, her head all a flutter.

'I'm having a sort of party later on. Do you want to come?' he asked smiling.

'Well I'd like to but...it's difficult,' she muttered, thinking about William at home.

'No buts. It's a date,' he said.

'I...no I can't. Really. I've already got something planned,' she said quickly.

'Well after the dance the other week I thought... you know. I'd become your number one priority.'

Liz blushed at the mention of their brief intimacy and became flustered. Excusing herself she disappeared into the kitchen. She leant against the worktop trying to regain control. Her mind was in a whirl, her heart beating wildly. She was at a crossroads in her life and she didn't know what to do.

At home her husband was clearly suffering from some form of stress disorder whereas in the bar was a fun guy offering the opportunity of excitement. Forbidden fruit, perhaps more. What should she do? What should she do? Risk having an affair and destroying their long term marriage? Well William clearly didn't think it was significant as he had dismissed their anniversary as being unimportant anyway.

She suddenly felt emboldened. What the hell. It would be fun and she could stop it going too far anyway. After all, he was only inviting her to a party. There would be lots of other people there too. She'd be OK, she convinced herself.

Liz strode out of the kitchen, her decision made. 'Sorry about that I had to check on something in the oven.'

'So long as it wasn't a bun,' he joked and regretted it immediately as she glowered at him.

'Well, have you decided whether you're coming to celebrate my birthday or not?'

'Yes, of course. It will be fun,' she heard herself say.

'That's great. Got to get back,' he said, looking at his watch. Quickly downing his pint he added, 'I'll pick you up if you like?'

'Well I'm not sure.' Liz's mind was in a whirl. Although he now knew where she lived, she couldn't get him to pick her up from home. 'Pick me up by the Rotunda,' she directed.

She felt a buzz of excitement and heard herself ask. 'What time?'

'That's great. How about 7.30?' He flashed a knowing smile at her. 'See you then.' Frank slipped off the stool and almost skipped joyfully to the door. 'See you later.'

As Liz gazed at the closing door she was already regretting her decision. What would she tell William?' she pondered.

Liz drove back home feeling excited by the prospect of a secret dalliance with Frank. His invitation to the birthday party made her feel wickedly coquettish. So on the way home when she stopped to buy him a birthday card she also bought herself some sexy underwear.

She was trying to be cool and downplay Frank's attention of her. But the common-sense part of her brain wasn't working. Instead she felt like a schoolgirl with a playground crush, flattered that someone was showing an interest in her.

'After all, William wasn't interested in her or anything else at the moment,' she argued. 'Well it wasn't like it was going to be a serious affair. Just a bit of fun. Yes, that's all. Just a bit of fun,' she convinced herself. She would go for a laugh.

Chapter 19

It took almost a week for William to get his composure back and feel strong enough to leave the flat.

During that time alone in the flat William's mood had worsened. He was full of self-pity. He couldn't sleep because the recording of Pete's final actions kept playing over and over in his head.

If only Pete had checked the wires himself as he usually did, rather than relying on Williams judgement, perhaps he'd be home celebrating the end of the campaign. Instead, Pete had trusted that William had accurately sussed it out. With disastrous consequences. The bomb maker had clearly got to understand the way they collaborated and had deliberately misled them.

He refused to seek any medical help or speak to any of his colleagues.

Now at last he felt 'human' enough to show an interest in their relationship. He picked up the anniversary card she'd given him a week previously and slowly ripped it open. His normally steady hands were still shaking as he slid his finger under the flap and pulled out the card.

Liz normally sent his cards to wherever he was posted. However, he'd told her of their return to the UK and possibly that he and the card might pass in transit, so she'd held on to it.

It was her normal humorous type of card. On the glossy front cover a cartoon woman with arms crossed standing by a toilet.

The words said '*You're my favourite husband so long as you leave the seat down and don't fart in your sleep*'.

He smiled. She had written inside. *All my love to my hero. Can't wait to get you home.* She'd obviously kissed the card and left an imprint of her lips in lipstick. He lifted it to his own and kissed the lip signature. He felt a pang of affection.

He recalled the other homecomings when they'd showered together and energetically made up for lost time, afterward dozing off in each other's arms in the marital bed. His recollections stirred some positivity in his mind and he vowed he would make up for the lost week.

The small flat was dark and gloomy and making him feel claustrophobic. He needed to get out and get some fresh air. Somehow his guilt was easier to bear.

He got dressed quickly and made his way to the front door. He looked in a small porcelain jar where Liz normally kept a spare front door key. As he dug into it he saw a shiny chain.

'She's obviously treated herself to a new bracelet,' he thought.

He pulled it out to admire it then saw the name 'Frank' engraved on it. He did a double take.

'What the hell! Is she two timing me?' he wondered. 'Perhaps she picked it up in the park. There's obviously a simple explanation, surely?'

He put the bracelet back into the jar and retrieved the spare key he'd been looking for.

He left the flat and walked into the town centre gloomily staring at the pavement, Pete's death and the mystery bracelet whirling through his mind.

It was a surreal feeling to be walking through the beautiful Montpellier gardens unarmed, whereas only a few weeks previously he had been armed to the hilt and constantly on alert for insurgents at every corner. He felt naked, exposed.

In this current genteel environment it was difficult to think that he had been doing delicate defusing jobs in impossibly hot desert temperatures with the threat of been shot at any time.

People were going about their business without an apparent care in the world. They didn't know or probably didn't care about the sacrifice that had been made in their name. He knew that out in the desert kids would still be stepping on IEDs, dying, losing limbs. The insurgents would continue their struggle to impose their preferred way of life. Nothing had changed, except Pete was dead and for what?

He made his way to the Copa bar in the blocked off Regent Street and ordered himself a pint of bitter. There was nothing like a pint of British beer from a pub. He had often met Liz there when she was working on a set at the nearby Everyman Theatre.

He carried his glass outside on to the terrace and watched the shoppers and workers in their lunchbreak scurrying back and forth.

The first pint went down and didn't touch the sides. He felt the beer buzz after he'd had only half a pint. He remembered he'd had little to eat during the day. So when he got the next pint he ordered a lasagne. He had no intention of getting wasted and wanted to be back home when Liz returned from the pub.

Perhaps he'd buy her the flowers he'd forgotten for their wedding anniversary and to say sorry for slapping her.

He felt ill at ease recalling the incident. He had never hit her before, but she'd goaded him by disrespecting Pete's death and...but what about the bracelet? His logical brain switched in. No, he mustn't jump to conclusions. There might be a perfectly understandable explanation.

After he'd finished his second pint and eaten the piping hot lasagne, he made his way to a flower stall in the Promenade and bought a bouquet of flowers for £30. As he carried the flowers through Imperial Gardens on his way back to the flat he felt very self-conscious. People looked at him. Women smiled. He wasn't sure if the flowers would help make up for his uncharacteristic assault on his wife. He hoped it would. He went back home and waited.

PART TWO

Excavation

Chapter 20

Frank made his way happily back to work pleased with himself and the prospect of a date with Liz. He was supposed to have completed digging six inspection holes for the surveyors to complete their site surveys. However, his 'unavoidable' delay due to the call of several pints and chatting Liz up in the pub had taken longer than he planned. After all, it was his birthday.

When he got back to the old airfield, his business partner Joe, was waiting for him and tamping mad.

'Where the hell have you been?' he demanded.

'What's it to do with you what I do in my lunch break?' Frank slurred, the beer buzz giving him courage.

'A lot. This job, this contract and my frigging house, that's what. We got the contract for geotechnical surveying because we've got a good reputation. I don't want you bleeding well jeopardising that. Remember, this is your firm as well as mine.'

'Alright, keep your frigging hair on. I'll finish it before they arrive.'

You'll never finish all of them and put the side supports in before they arrive. I should have never trusted your judgement.'

'Look, if you get out of my way and stop whinging I can get on with it.'

At which stage he pushed the other out of the way and climbed into his JCB.

'You'll be the death of me you will,' Joe shouted over the top of the revving engine. 'I want it done by four o'clock and don't stray off the marks. There are high pressure oil and water pipes down there. We don't want any more disasters. The insurance company won't cover us again if you cock up.'

'Oh piss off and let me get on,' Frank shouted, annoyed that his happiness was being overshadowed by this petty work issue. 'The more you talk, the less I'll get done.'

'Four o'clock, hear me? Joe shouted, 'And don't get pissing off before I bring them back here.'

'Yes, yes. Now get out the way.'

As Joe disappeared off site Frank went into hyper drive to complete his tasks in time using the back hoe to dig out the holes and by 3:45 he was nearing his target.

'There you go my son. Five holes done and sides shored up. Just a few more shovels of this final one and the jobs a good 'un'. I think we can get away without shoring this one. Although I got to admit the ground does look a bit soggy. I'm sure it'll be firm enough for them to do their quick inspection. I ain't got time now if they're coming back for four.'

As he manoeuvred the bucket for the final time, the hoe scrapped against something.

'Oh what the hell was that? Isn't that always the way.'

Frank gazed into the hole and at the bottom he spotted a large metal object that his digging had uncovered.

'Oh shit!' Don't say there's an unmarked pipe down there. I'm sure I'm in the right place...unless he marked it out wrong of course. Oh balls, I'd have completed it in ten minutes too.'

At that moment his mobile rang; he recognised Joe's number. 'Yes, hello Joe. What is it? Yes it's me...yes I've nearly done...what, what do you mean they can't make it today? I've worked like a ding-bat to get this lot done.'

Although he made a token protest he was actually feeling a great sense of relief that he could examine whatever it was he had unearthed.

'Oh, by the way Joe...Joe you still there? Bleeding useless phone...crap signal around here...Hello, oh he's gone. All that rushing around and they won't be coming until tomorrow after all,' he bleated.

Before he put his phone away he decided to send a text message to Liz.

'*Enjoyed the kiss, look forward 2 more 2nite. See you at 7.30. LOL Frank xxx*'

Smiling to himself, he put the phone into his back pocket.

What Frank didn't know was that Liz had left her mobile at the flat on charge.

'Well I suppose the pubs still open.' Frank thought, looking at his watch. 'Although the lovely Liz only works til three. Whatever, I'll make up for it tonight,' he said, already fantasising about their next encounter.

'I suppose I'd better see what's down here first. Hopefully it's just an old oil drum they used for refuelling the planes.'

Frank dropped an aluminium ladder into the 10 feet deep hole and climbed down with a spade to examine the mysterious object. He was surprised to feel the bottom of the ladder sink down into mud as he climbed down. Clearly the ground was marshier than he thought. As he alighted from the ladder he noted several of the rungs had disappeared into the ooze.

He squelched his way the short distance to the cylindrical metal 'pipe' and carefully scraped his spade along its length to expose more of it.

'Funny angle for a pipe...It's probably just a bit of scrap ...what's that noise?' he wondered, listening intently. 'Sounds like ticking...it's only my watch you donut...yeah but my watch is digital...dhurr!' he chided himself. 'Well unless somebody's buried a clock down here...what else makes a ticking noise? Jesus! It can't be...surely, not a bomb? Christ a bomb!' he said, backing away from it.

'No it can't be! It wasn't on the bomb survey,' he argued. 'Well, if it is, I need to get my arse out of here pronto.'

Quickly he galvanised himself into action and rushed to the ladder. He started climbing rapidly up out of the hole.

Suddenly he felt the ladder start to move from its forty five degree angle to the vertical. Initially he thought Joe had returned to site and was messing about. He looked up and to his horror saw that the mud supporting the top of the ladder was caving in. It was pushing the ladder backwards.

Frank hung on desperately as it went beyond vertical and hit the opposite side of the hole. The sudden jolt dislodged his fingers and he fell almost on top of the suspected bomb.

As the landslip continued to pour mud into the hole he was conscious of the JCB also moving dangerously forward, threatening to fall into the hole as the ground moved underneath it. The weight of it had obviously stressed the edge of the top soil.

'God, perhaps I should have shored it up after all,' Frank thought irrationally.

Too late. The earth continued to avalanche into the hole. The weight of the landslip was bending the aluminium ladder which was now pushing on his chest.

Winded by the fall and the tightening compression on his chest Frank frantically scrabbled to his feet to get higher up.

'God, I'm being buried alive…effing hell.'

The avalanche of mud continued, the weight of it pushing on his chest restricting his breathing and he blacked out.

Chapter 21

Liz descended the steps to the flat still desperately thinking about a convincing lie to tell William about where she was going that evening.

She had never done anything like this before in all the long years of their marriage.

She was further wrong footed by William's total change of temperament, for as she opened the door, he was standing in front of her with a forced smile and a bunch of flowers. Whereas when she left him earlier he was still very down.

She was now overwhelmed by guilt about Frank's invitation.

'Hello, darling. I'm sorry about my miserable face over the last week. Will you forgive me?' he grovelled, offering her the flowers.

'I…I, well…yes…yes of course,' she said completely overwhelmed.

'I've made a reservation for a special anniversary meal tonight. I hope you haven't got any other plans,' he continued. I'm so sorry about… you know slapping you. Please forgive me. I will never do it again.'

Liz was reminded of her anger but took the bouquet from him and slowly looked at the flowers and then at him.

'I tell you this,' she said, her stomach screwed up in anger. 'I won't be treated like those women on army bases that end up as punch bags. I can't say I understand the trauma of being in a war zone. But I do know that domestic violence is not an excuse for it.'

'No. I know and I wouldn't expect you to. It was just…you touched a raw nerve and I'm desperately sorry.' His eyes brimmed.

He tried to hold her hand but she turned her back on him and slumped down on the settee putting the flowers beside her.

'You know when we first met, you really swept me off my feet,' Liz explained, 'I used to think you were so…so sweet. A real macho man. I never thought I'd end up getting close to you, let alone marrying you.'

'I know it hasn't been easy for you with me doing the job I do. But it's worked ok for the last decade or so hasn't it?' William said, sitting beside her.

'Has it?' Liz questioned. 'We're like an old married couple who are too familiar with each other. The excitement wears off. The magic dies and you take each other for granted. And you're hardly at home.'

'You knew what service life would be like. We discussed this before we got married.'

'I know we did But I didn't appreciate what it would mean.'

'So what are you saying? You've had enough of me… of this marriage. Is that what you're saying? Well, is it?' he insisted. 'Is that why you've got another man in your life?' he probed.

'Another man! What do you mean?' Liz said, uncomfortably.

'In the little jar by the door. There's a gold bracelet with the name of Frank on it.'

'Oh that...that...' Liz shifted anxiously on the settee.' I umm...had trouble with the drains. I had a flood in here. There was a blockage and... um one of the pub customers offered to sort it out for me. He took his bracelet off and we thought we'd lost it. I wondered where it went,' she said, withholding the full story. Liz was beginning to feel as if things were unravelling and her dalliance was about to be exposed.

'So where do we go from here?' William asked.

'Well I've made plans for this evening,' she informed him. 'I was expecting you to be in bed for the next couple of days and I...didn't want to disturb you. So I...'

'But I've been away for a long time,' William pleaded.

'Yes. But you're not the William I know,' Liz said firmly. 'When he comes back, I might still be here.' Liz amazed herself at her boldness. Perhaps she was moving on after all.

Chapter 22

Joe returned to site to discuss the revised timetable with Frank but couldn't immediately see him.

'Well, there's the JCB, but where is he? Bleeding typical, I bet he's pissed off again, just as I thought.'

Joe walked towards the JCB, passing the excavations which Frank had completed.

'Well I suppose at least he's dug and shored up these,' he observed.

As he arrived by the JCB he was dismayed at what he saw. 'Christ, he's left this right on the side of the hole. Any minute now it could fall in. The useless idiot.'

'Dammit, look at the state of this one,' he cursed, as he peered into the collapsed hole. 'It looks like it's collapsed and he's buggered up the ladder as well. Oh for Chrissake!' he said in exasperation. 'You want a job doing. Do it yourself. I'll give him what for when I get hold of him. I bet he went straight back down the pub as soon as I told him they weren't coming today. No wonder he hung up so fast.'

Frank regained consciousness. He was having difficulty breathing. There was a great weight on his chest. Fortunately, the ladder which had bent under the weight of the landslip, had also protected him from being completely crushed.

'Oh god,' he groaned. 'My chest hurts. Where am I?' There was a ticking noise. Was he in his bedroom? It was dark underneath the mud cocoon. Pitch black in fact. Was it night time?

Slowly he recalled what had happened. The hole… the ladder…the collapse. He must be buried. As his senses cleared, he suddenly recalled the bomb.

'Jesus…the bomb…shit I can hear it ticking…'

Suddenly the gravity of the situation hit him. A wave of panic washed over him. He felt claustrophobic. He was going to die, buried alive and nobody would know where he was.

'Come on. You can handle this. You're not a babbie. You can do this,' he repeated, berating himself.

He assessed his physical health. Apart from the weight on his chest and a dull pain in his leg, generally he felt as well as he could, given the present circumstances.

'At least I don't think I've broken anything, thank Christ. Hopefully it's just bruised.'

His arms had been forced back against the excavated wall behind him in a 'hands up' posture. It was as if he was surrendering to the vicious onslaught.

He could feel the closeness of the dirt in front of his face, his breath bouncing back at him.

'I wonder if I can just move my arms and clear some space in front of my face?' he asked himself, flexing his arms.

His efforts were rewarded with a shower of more dirt which cascaded down on to his face. He quickly closed his eyes and shook his head to dislodge a lump of mud that had slipped down and rested against his chin.

'Ugh, uck,' he spluttered, spitting the dirt off his lips. Again he flexed his biceps and his efforts allowed some movement of his arms and hands. Slowly, by moving his wrist in a waving motion, he dislodged more dirt and gained some more space. But the earth prison appeared to be solid.

Irrationally he thought, 'this must be what it's like to be trapped under an avalanche in the snow.'

He opened his eyes again, still unable to get his hands to his face. He flittered his eyelids to get rid of the fine earth that had settled on them and shook his head to remove the dirt that had again cascaded down on to his face.

Slowly, he was able to bring his arms from their 'surrender position' down by his side; his fingers frantically digging through the mixture of clay and loose soil until he could wriggle his hands in front of him. Carefully he felt around in the darkness. He touched something metallic. It was the buckled aluminium ladder which was squashing his chest.

'If I can just move this a bit I might be able to breathe easier,' he groaned. He pushed against the ladder. But nothing moved. He tried again, putting all his efforts into shoving.

'M-o-v-e you bastard,' he strained. Stars filled his head as a reward for his efforts.

Nothing moved.

Again he tried. 'M—o—v—e,' he demanded, putting every ounce of his strength into a mighty heave.

This time his efforts were rewarded with another cascade of soil as the ladder moved a fraction and took some slight pressure off his chest.

Exhausted by his efforts, he took stock of his situation.

'Hopefully,' he thought, 'Joe will be back here in a minute and he'll find me.'

Above ground, Joe had made a decision. 'I'd better move the JCB before we lose it in the hole as well. God he's piggin' useless,' Joe continued, muttering to himself. 'I wonder if he's bothered to lock it?'

Joe climbed up the steps of the machine and tried the door. To his annoyance it opened. Climbing into the cab he was further infuriated to see the keys in place.

'Jesus, he was in such a bleedin' hurry to get to the pub that he's even left the keys in the ignition. Anybody could have nicked it.'

Joe fired up the JCB and revved the engine.

Underground, Frank heard the JCB start up and assumed that Joe was on site. Frantically he started shouting. 'JOE, JOE. JOE I'M DOWN HERE,' he yelled at the top of his voice. 'HELP! THE HOLES COLLAPSED. JOE, DOWN HERE. ITS ME, FRANK.'

But shut in the cab and with the engine noise, Joe couldn't hear and Frank's cries went unheard.

Unused to driving the JCB, initially Joe selected the wrong gear and it lurched backwards towards the edge of the hole, the backhoe precariously nudging some more of the mudslide.

Realising his mistake and with his 'heart in his mouth', he slammed on the powerful brakes and jiggled with the gear lever to select the forward gear. In his haste he stamped on the accelerator and the giant wheels spun on the collapsing terrain causing it to lurch quite violently. Joe, fearing that it was going to fall into the hole, was seriously contemplating having to leap out.

'Come on you bastard,' Joe shouted at the bucking machine, egging it on as if it was a misbehaving animal.

At last, Joe gained control and coaxed the machine away from the edge of the hole spitting more earth into the collapsed excavation as it moved.

'Gently does it,' he encouraged.

Meanwhile, trapped in his underground prison, Frank could hear the noise of Joe's battle with his digger and felt the vibrations through the soil. Apprehensively he waited, expecting any minute to hear it falling into the hole and being crushed by the additional 800 kilo weight.

He closed his eyes as more dirt cascaded on top of the pile of mud above him and he waited fearfully.

After moving the JCB far enough away from the hole, Joe killed the engine and locked it. Climbing down, he went back to inspect the damage to the edge of the hole.

'Bugger. What a mess! Well, we'll just have to have another go at that tomorrow, if I can find that bleeding Frank that is,' he muttered, crossly.

In the meantime, Frank had dug more fallen dirt away from his face and started calling again.

'JOE, JOE. I'M DOWN HERE. I'M IN THE HOLE. HELP JOE HELP.' The hole colluded against him and absorbed his voice preventing it from escaping. His cries for help just bounced off the dirt wall in front of him.

Joe was 'tamping mad' with his missing partner and had returned to his car to go to the pub and remonstrate with him.

Frank faintly heard Joe start his car and his hope of rescue faded.

'JOE, HELP. I'M DOWN HERE. IN THE HOLE. JOE HELP,' he repeated hopelessly, his throat raw from his repeated distress call.

He paused to hear for any response. Nothing.

The silence was broken only by the rasping of Frank's breath and the ticking of the bomb beside him. The landslip had dumped Frank right by the side of it.

'Oh god, if I don't suffocate then I shall be blown up. Nobody will know what happened to me,' Frank whined dramatically. His spirits nose-dived.

However, instead of dashing off to the pub, Joe had only driven the short distance to the site entrance and decided to phone Frank. 'Why didn't I think about this before?' he castigated himself.

After punching in Frank's number, he was gratified to hear it ringing out…'Come on Frank answer the bleedin thing,' he said impatiently. 'Where the hell are you?'

Frank was startled by the vibration from his back pocket as Joe's call rang his mobile. 'Jesus, I thought that was the bomb then,' he said his heart racing. 'Why the hell didn't I think of using it before?' he reproached himself.

His next problem was attempting to retrieve it from his back pocket. The additional dirt had filled in the void that he'd been able to make. Slowly and methodically he manoeuvred his right hand away from the ladder and tried to move it the short distance behind him to his back pocket and the vibrating phone.

On the surface, Joe's patience had run out as it tripped into Frank's voice mail. 'Frank, I don't know where the hell you are, but get your arse back to site pronto.' Joe stabbed the red button and ended the call.

The vibrations in Frank's back pocket stopped. 'Shit, he's hung up. If I can…get…to…it,' he encouraged himself, 'then I can…get help.'

With great difficulty, he moved his buttocks away from the excavated wall far enough to slide his hand along it towards his pocket.

'Nearly there, just a bit more… ' His fingers gripped the edge of the phone. 'Oh that's it. Now can I prise it out of my pocket….slowly…slowly,' he coaxed. 'Right, got it now.'

As he withdrew, it he wondered if it would work anyway. He knew the signal was pretty intermittent on the site and underneath several feet of mud and dirt it was probably a hopeless wish. Then again, he reasoned, if he could receive a call, surely he'd be able to make one. Wouldn't he?

'Now if I can get my arm back round…must stop…' The exertion of moving his arm through the sea of loose dirt was exhausting and made him hot and breathless…'. catch my breath.'

Abruptly the ticking stopped. 'Thank God for that,' he thought.

However, he suddenly realised that this might signal the detonation phase.

'Oh my god, is this where I kiss my arse goodbye?' he muttered, the weight of silent anticipation heavy on his mind. After what seemed an eternity nothing happened. He breathed a sigh of relief.

'I need to get the phone up to my face and call Joe.'

But his arm was jammed again. He started twisting it sideways to help free it. The trick worked. His arm was becoming loose. 'Gently…gently,' he whispered, using every ounce of concentration he could muster.

Suddenly the pressure on his chest increased as more soil slipped into the excavation. 'Shit, that ladder hurts. It's sticking into my ribs again.'

The voice in his head told him '*concentrate on the phone.*'

But after the initial movement, his arm got jammed again. Try as he might, it wouldn't move any further in the small gap he had created, because he was now holding the phone.

'Just like a monkey trap,' he thought, 'drop the banana or you get caught!'

No matter what he tried, it wouldn't move. 'Oh shit. It's stuck.' The position of his arm was cutting off the blood flow to his hand.

'Bugger, I've got pins and needles in my arm now. Don't let go of the phone, don't let go off the phone,' he repeated the mantra. But after a few minutes the loss of circulation made him lose feeling in his fingers and he could feel the phone slipping out of his grasp.

'Oh no, not now I've got it this far. Please God, don't let me…' but it was gone. The panic returned. There was not much air in the small void he'd created and now he realised he was hyperventilating.

Then he faintly heard the car pull away and knew he was now really on his own. It was now down to him to get himself out of the mess. But how?

Chapter 23

Joe went straight to the Flying Machine, where Frank had been drinking earlier. He made his way through the small corridor to the large public bar. It was virtually empty. He knew Frank wouldn't be in the Lounge bar. It was not his style.

'George, have you seen Frank?' he asked the Landlord.

'You mean the birthday boy? No, not since dinner time. Liz tells me he was in a bit of a hurry, almost didn't finish his last pint.'

'Oh yeah,' Joe said sceptically. 'Are you sure you're not covering for him. The bugger's disappeared from site.'

'You know what he's like. He's probably got a 'bit' he's taken behind those old sheds. Although, he was chatting to Liz earlier on, but she didn't leave until a long time after Frank.'

'Yeah, you're probably right. But if he does come back here tell him to give me a call, urgently.'

'Why don't you call him?'

'I've tried. He ain't answering his phone.'

'Oh OK, will do.'

Joe made his way back to his car, racking his brains as to where his missing partner might have gone as he punched in his mobile number again muttering to himself.

The phone rang out. Joe was impatient and muttered under his breath. 'Where the hell are you Frank?'

Back in the collapsed hole, Frank heard his mobile vibrating and ringing again.

'Oh shit, that made me jump. Where the hell is it? If I can just…move…my hand again and feel around … perhaps it's not dropped down too far.'

With a lot of effort he pushed his hand down through the dirt until his fingers touched the vibrating phone and it immediately stopped ringing.

'Shit They've hung up,' he groaned. His sprits fell.

At the other end of the call Joe was just about to hang up when it was answered. 'Oh he's answered! At last. Frank, where the bleedin' hell are you? You idle assed sod. I've been looking all over for you…Frank… FRANK!'

In the hole Frank could hear a tinny voice,

'I must have answered it. HELLO CAN YOU HEAR ME?' he shouted excited with this sudden change of fortune. Perhaps all was not lost after all.

'Frank, FRANK is that you? You sound very distant. Get your hand out of that woman's knickers and stop pratting around.'

'HELLO, I CAN'T HEAR YOU…WHOEVER IT IS, YOU'VE GOT TO HELP ME,' Frank shouted.

'Frank, stop pissing around and pick up the phone and talk properly.'

'HELP, YOU'VE GOT TO HELP ME…I'M STUCK IN THIS HOLE.

'I can't hear what you're saying…you'll have to speak up,' Joe shouted at the phone.

'It's no good I can't hear what you're saying. JOE, IF THAT'S YOU...YOU'VE GOT TO HELP ME...I'M AT THE SITE...'

'Frank, if that's you, I can't hear you. We must have a dodgy line. I'll call you again.'

'THE HOLE...I'M TRAPPED IN THE HOLE,' Frank yelled at the top of his voice.

'It's no good, I'll try calling again. I can't hear a word,' Joe repeated and 'cleared' the call.

'NO, DON'T HANG UP... '.Frank pleaded. He heard the call clear. 'Shit.' His hopes dashed again.

Joe punched in the numbers again but immediately got the message *'The number you are calling is not available.'*

He tried again several times with the same result and eventually gave up and drove back to his small office.

In the meantime, Frank was trying to grab the phone again. 'If only I could get the phone ...' All the while, he was frantically moving his fingers to capture the errant mobile but just as he thought he'd got it, the mobile slid out of his grasp again. It slithered out of reach down a small void on to the floor of the excavation clanking against the bomb casing as it fell.

'Shit, shit, shit,' Frank exploded. 'I can't take much more of this, I'm either going to be blown up or be suffocated in this hell hole.'

Joe finished off the paperwork in the office and popped in to his 'local pub' on the way home. One of the customers was Frank's landlady at his B & B.

'Hi Joe, how's the job going?' she said sitting at the bar stool next to him.

'Yeah OK. Well, at least it was until Frank decided to slip off early.'

'Oh you can't begrudge him that after all it is his birthday. Bless him.'

'So long as he doesn't cock-up our contract, no I suppose not,' Joe said sternly.

'Has he gone somewhere nice?' she asked.

'I thought you might know.'

'No, I haven't seen him. He would normally dive in for a bath before he hit the town,' the landlady informed him.

You ain't seen him then?'

'No, not this afternoon. He's probably gone back to the pub.'

'No I tried there.' Joe advised her.

'What about that woman he's been chatting up?'

'Yeah, I suppose he might be with her,' Joe conceded.

'But then he would have had to come home to 'doll himself up' if he's on a date,' the woman suggested.

'Yeah I suppose.'

'You want me to give him a call?' she asked.

'Well I've already called him several times with no luck.' Joe thought about her suggestion for a minute. 'Yeah I suppose, he might answer it if he knows that it's from you. He might be pissed off with me and rejecting my calls for the bollocking I gave him earlier.'

The landlady removed the phone from her bag and called Frank's number. She listened for a second. 'No, it's gone straight into his voicemail.'

'Ok, well thanks for trying anyway. That's another theory down the tubes.' Joe had another thought. 'Cynth, was Frank's car at home?'

'No. He drove it off this morning.'

'I didn't spot it on the site. Then again I was so angry. The only thing I saw was the mess he'd made of one of the holes he promised me he'd complete. You want another drink before I go?' he asked her.

'That's very kind,' she said emptying her glass. 'A Bacardi and coke, thanks.'

Joe left the pub wondering what the hell had happened to Frank, 'but he's a grown man. I'm sure he'll turn up tomorrow boasting of some conquest or other.'

Chapter 24

A group of four bored 14 year old school kids pushed through the broken chain link fence surrounding the industrial site, keen to see what was going on there.

'Look, they've only dug some holes that's all. Nothing interesting. Come on, let's go over the playing field instead,' the spikey haired one suggested.

'Yeah, come on,' one of the others agreed.

Just as they started to leave they spotted the yellow digging machine where Joe had parked it.

'Hey look, there's that JCB; it's still here.'

'Have you seen that You Tube video of the dancing JCBs?'

'You what? Dancing JCBs! No way.'

'Way" It's great. See, they got this line of them doing stuff set to music. Going up on the back hoes.'

'Back hoes?'

'Yeah, that digging arm at the back of it.'

'Hey, do you reckon we can do something like that? Let's see if we can get in to it,' the spikey haired one encouraged. The group ran over to the machine and he climbed up and tried the door.

'Nah, the doors locked. Give us that lump of metal,' He ordered.

'What you going to do?'

'Smash the glass.'

'What if it's alarmed?'

'Then we piss off real quick.'

One of the others found a bent reinforcing bar and gave it to him. It took several attempts but finally he smashed the glass on driver's door and pushed his way into the cab.

'Hey, that's not fair. I want a go,' a pimply face youth demanded.

'I'm driving. It was my idea.' The spikey haired yob announced. 'Looks like nobody's driving anyway,' he told them, after looking around. 'There's no keys in the ignition.'

'Can you hot wire it?'

'Don't know. Never done one before. I could try. I suppose.'

In the meantime one of the others had spotted Frank's car.

'Hey over here. Behind that portaloo. It's a Renault 19.'

'Bit old though ain't?'

'Yeah, but its 16 valve and pretty fast for its age. I know how to hot wire one of them, come on.'

The spikey haired one leapt down from the JCB and ran over to Frank's car.

'Yeah, but don't they have immobilisers fitted?' the pimply faced one asked.

'We'll soon find out,' the spikey haired youth said breathlessly. He pulled open the driver's door ready to start the key bypass 'modification', when he spotted the keys still where Frank had left them. In the ignition.

'Yeah, we're in luck. The geezers left the keys for us.'

'Brilliant, jump aboard, we're going for a spin.'

The others quickly scrambled into the car and almost before they had closed the doors, he started the engine. He stamped heavily on the accelerator and it leapt forward spitting stones from its wildly spinning tyres.

'This one's got multi-point fuel injection. They reckon it can do 130 mph,' the spikey haired driver informed them as he attempted a handbrake turn.

The others derided his failed attempt.

'Call that a handbrake turn? Let me have a go,' the youth in the passenger seat beside him shouted.

'Sod off. I was just getting used to the car,' he said, this time executing a perfect ninety degree side slide.' See,' he boasted. 'Perfect.'

This gave him confidence in handling the car and the speed hurtling around the site duly increased.

He was racing around the site using the holes that Frank had dug as the handbrake turning points when they spotted someone taking an interest in the proceedings.

'Look, there's somebody over there being nosey. Keep your head down. I think it's my next door neighbour. I don't want him to see me,' the front seat passenger warned, pulling his hoodie up.

'He's alright,' the driver assured. 'He's not interested in us. Just taking the dog for a walk, that's all.'

However, distracted by looking over at the dog walker the driver missed his turning point and yelled, 'Sod it. Hang on.'

He jammed on the brakes but it was too late. All four wheels locked on the muddy ground and they headed directly to one of the holes.

The occupants braced for the inevitable crash. The car had scrubbed off little forward momentum before it nose-dived down10 feet at about 30mph. The impact demolished the front end of the car as it hit the far side excavation. Clouds of steam immediately rose up from the smashed radiator.

'Is everybody alright?' the shocked driver called, as he struggled to open his door.

'Shit man. You could have killed us.'

'I bumped my head,' one of the others groaned.

The driver finally decided to exit via the smashed door window.

'Bloody hell, you maniac. It's going to catch fire,' the front seat passenger shouted as he clambered out through the buckled door.

'I banged my knees you prat,' one of the back seat passengers moaned.

'It's going to catch fire. Look at that smoke,' the fourth youth called rushing to get out.

'Its steam you idiot. Don't you know nuffin?' the driver called, clambering up on to the car's roof and out of the hole.

'Come on, we got to get out of here before they call the Police.'

'I can smell petrol,' the fourth youth volunteered.

'Yeah, dummy. It's because it's got a petrol engine. What else would you smell?' the driver derided, watching the others climb up the car.

'Quick, get out before it catches fire.'

The dog walker rushed over to them. 'Oh my god! Are you alright? That was a terrible crash. I've called the Fire brigade and the Police. Is everybody out?'

'Come on Tom,' the spikey haired leader called, grabbing the fourth youths arm and moving away from the dog walker.

'You can't leave. You must wait for the Police,' the dog walker insisted.

Ignoring the dog walkers protestations, the group ran off and now having got over the initial shock they started laughing at the near disaster.

'Come back you little sods,' the dog walker shouted at the fleeing youths. Behind him there was a mighty 'vroomph' as the car caught fire. Quickly he backed away from the inferno as plumes of black toxic smoke rose into the air.

The Fire and Rescue service arrived on site within ten minutes of the call, but by then the car was pretty well gutted.

The fire chief interrogated the dog walker. 'Were there any occupants in the car?'

'No I don't think so. Four of them came out and ran off. So I assume that was all there were.'

'Joyriders again,' the Fire chief tutted. 'Anyway, these bloody holes are dangerous. There's no guarding around them. Anybody could fall into them. Do you know who's responsible for the site?'

'No I don't. But there's a JCB over there. Perhaps it's got a telephone number on it.'

'I'll get one of my lads to check and ask control to give them a call. Somebody ought to put guard rails around these holes,' he repeated.

Chapter 25

The telephone number on the side of the JCB was indeed Joe's, and, alerted by the Fire and Rescue chief, he quickly arrived on site.

The fire chief explained his requirement to put guarding up around the holes.

'Yeah, well, I'll put some rails up but nobody should be on the site anyway. Its private property and we're preparing it for development,' Joe replied looking at the smoking wreck of the car. 'Christ, that car's a mess. Anybody hurt?'

'No. Joyriders got hold of it and crashed it. Luckily they all got out before it went up in flames. I'm not sure that guard rails would have helped, but we've got to safeguard anybody else who walks through here,' the Fire chief advised.

'Oh, alright. As I said they shouldn't be here in the first place,' Joe insisted indignantly.

'Thanks. But duty of care and all that. You've even got to look after the vandals these days, I'm afraid.'

'Even bleedin Joyriders? God! Whats the world coming to? Well whoever's car that was won't be having any joy will they? What was it?'

'A Renault 19, I think.'

'You could have fooled me.' Joe said in disbelief, looks at the rusty wreck.

'Yes, we think so.'

'What a mess!'

'We've dragged it out of the hole to make sure we've extinguished it completely.

Suddenly 'the penny dropped'. 'A Renault 19! No surely not!' Joe exclaimed.

'What. You think you might know the owner?' the fire chief quizzed.

'Oh my god. I think it could be my partner's car.'

'Well here's whats left of the number plate.' The fire chief showed him the charred plate he'd been holding.

'Oh my god! Yes. That's it. It's his car.'

'Does your partner always leave his car with keys in the ignition for joyriders to help themselves?'

'What?'

'Yes, the keys were in the ignition.'

'He does leave them in the car…But only when he's around. Usually even on site, he's never very far from it,' Joe said, wracking his brains to try and remember the sequence of events. 'He was here just before four… but when I came back about quarter past he wasn't anywhere to be seen. I thought he was getting his 'leg over' somewhere…but now I'm not so sure. What hole did you find the car in?'

'That one there,' the Fire chief said, pointing at a nearby hole.

'God, it's full of water,' Joe blurted.

'Difficult to put the fire out without using water sir,' the Fireman said patiently.

'Oh my god…what a fool… Frank must have been here all the time…he would never go off site and leave the car with the keys in…Quickly check all the holes,'

136

Joe shouted, becoming animated. 'Let me think. Now where was the JCB when I moved it?'

Joe ran over to the JCB and spotted the damaged glass. 'Those little bastards have smashed the glass on this…now don't be distracted,' He told himself.

'Just a second Sir, what's going on?' the Fire Officer asked puzzled.

'My partner has been missing all afternoon.'

'Yes, I got that bit. So what makes you think he's in one of these holes?'

'I don't know, I can't think of anywhere else he could be…'

'Well if he was in the one where the car crashed, if the crash didn't kill him the fire or the water would have.'

'Thanks for those comforting words…'Joe said looking around wild eyed.

'So you haven't spoken to him since just before four?' the Fire officer probed.

'I think I contacted him once, but he was very faint. I've tried ringing his mobile again, but it just rings out or goes to his voicemail.'

'But it rings out first?' the Fire chief queried.

'Yes. Occasionally. The signal round here is crap.'

'Well, let's try and locate him from that,' the Fire chief suggested.

'As I say, the signal around here is pretty intermittent though.' Joe repeated anxiously.

'Well, it's a slim chance but we've got to try it. Right guys, can you spread out around all these holes and let's get some quiet on site. Turn the pumps off and turn your radios down. OK. So you're listening for a mobile ringing,' he instructed them. 'Right. You want to call him?' he asked Joe, as the firemen reached their positions.

'OK.' Joe selected Frank's number and was relieved to hear that it was ringing out. 'It's ringing,' he shouted.

'OK guys, ears to the ground... Anybody got anything?' the Fire Chief said, scanning the group.

A chorus of No's and then one of the Firemen on the far side of the site indicated that he'd heard something.

'I thought I did, but it's stopped,' he announced.

'Yeah. It's just gone in to voicemail,' Joe informed them, 'I'll call again.' He tamped the keys on his mobile again and listened. 'Damn, no signal. I told you it was pretty crappy around here.'

'Just keep trying,' the Fire chief encouraged calmly.

After the fifth attempt, Joe got a signal again and informed the listeners that it was ringing.

The fireman who thought he'd heard something had taken his helmet off and was lying on the ground listening intently. 'Yes definitely something coming over here. It's very faint but it sounds like... Dido singing 'White Flag?' he said, as if not believing his ears.

'Brilliant. Yes that's it,' Joe said joyfully. 'That's his ring tone.' Joe rushed over but stopped short as he remembered the collapsed excavation. 'Oh my God, he's going to be very lucky if he has survived under that lot,' he said dramatically. 'Yes, that's where the JCB was,' he recalled. 'Look at the mess I made moving it away from the hole. Shit. I might even have killed him sending more soil down there.'

'Now come on. We don't know for definite he's down there yet., It might just be his phone,' the Fire chief said quietly.

'Well, there's the top of the ladder. He probably used it to climb down,' Joe pointed out.

'We need to shore up the hole before we start doing anything. That soil is very loose. Have you got anything we can use?' he asked Joe.

'Yeah, over there by that shed. There should be some props, boards and a trench support,' Joe said pointing towards it.

'Thanks. That's the number one priority, then. Shore up the hole.'

'Frank…Frank…are you down there?' Joe shouted at the pile of mud.

Frank had been drifting in and out of consciousness for some time as the air in his cocoon became heavy with carbon dioxide. However, he surfaced from his 'coma' as he heard his name called.

'Am I dead? Is that you mother?' Frank called, his voice hoarse from several hours of unanswered yelling for help.

'Frank,' Joe called again.' Are you OK?'

Clarity of thought overcame Frank's lethargy caused by his cramped 'imprisonment.' He suddenly realised it was not a dream. It was not his dead Mother's voice. The pain across his chest, in his leg and around his back reminded him he was very much still alive.

It was his partner calling him. 'Joe, Joe, I'm down here,' he croaked. 'Joe, I'm down here…' he repeated. 'I'm trapped. Help me, please.'

'Frank, if you can hear me, I have the fire and rescue service with me.' Suddenly the volume of Joe's voice increased, the fire service having given him a megaphone to use. 'CAN YOU REACH THE LADDER AND KNOCK ON IT TO LET ME KNOW YOU'RE OK?'

Frank struggled to move his arm through the dirt and pushed his hand forward until he felt the hard metal of the ladder. And with great effort, he balled his fist, flexed his wrist and hit the aluminium strut several times.

On the surface all had gone quiet as they waited expectantly for a response.
'Clang, clang.'
A loud cheer went up as they heard the faint response.
'Oh thank god,' Joe said almost reverently. 'Quick, he's alive. We need to get him out. Now.'
'That hole is pretty dangerous. The side could go any minute,' The Fire chief cautioned.
'Come on,' Joe urged. 'We haven't got a moment to spare. He's been down there for several hours now. The mud could be suffocating him.'
'Listen, before we do anything, we need, props, excavation gear, a rescue tender, floodlighting and an ambulance,' reasoned the Fire chief.
'We can't afford to wait for all that. This is a race against time if we're going to bring him out alive. Bugger it. If you're not going to do it, I will.' Joe stood up and moved towards the top of the ladder.
As if to emphasise the gravity of the situation, the edge of the hole, where Joe had moved to, started giving way and sent another miniature earth slide into the hole.
'Keep away from the edge of the hole until we've got something to stand on,' the Fire chief told everyone.

'He's lasted this long. We don't want to be the cause of his demise now.'

'What an idiot!' Joe declared, putting his hands to his head.' I should have realised he was down there when I came back to site. Instead of bollocking him, I could have rescued him hours ago. Oh what a prat! Why wasn't I more observant?'

'No good blaming yourself Sir. That won't help. What's your partner's name?'

'Frank, Frank Schmidt.'

'Unusual name!'

'Yeah, I think his father was German.'

'FRANK, FRANK CAN YOU HEAR ME? MY NAME IS PAUL. I'M THE FIRE CHIEF HERE. WE'RE GOING TO GET YOU OUT. YOU'LL NEED TO REMAIN QUITE STILL WHILE WE'RE MOVING THE MUD AND DIRT...BUT WE'LL HAVE YOU OUT AS SOON AS POSSIBLE...CAN YOU HEAR ME?'

'Clank, clank.'

'Good...Can you drive the JCB, Joe?'

'Yeah.'

'Why don't you help the firemen bring some planks over here? That'll keep your mind occupied.'

'Yeah OK. Good idea.' Joe dragged himself away from the hole and ran back to the JCB, got the keys out of his pocket and fired it up. He drove to where the shoring gear was and the firemen quickly loaded large planks into the bucket.

'There you go boss. Here's the floodlights,' said another fireman placing a tripod upon which were surmounted several halogen lights. 'I'll just switch them on,' he said running back to a generator that he'd unloaded off the fire engine.

As the lights shone into every crevice of the hole, the Fire Chief was able to fully assess the task. 'Christ what a mess...it's a bleeding miracle he hasn't already suffocated. Can we get some air down to him?' he asked, looking at one of his team. The other nodded. 'There's a gap by the side of the ladder, look. Strip one of those Breathing Apparatus packs down and let's blow some air down to him.'

'OK skip,' the other responded, and set off to the Fire engine to undertake the necessary mods. As he did so, another vehicle arrived.

Chapter 26

'Oh well talk of the devil. Here's the Specialist Rescue Unit,' the Fire chief said looking, towards the approaching vehicle.

Doors slammed as the team exited the vehicle and the Leader was directed to Paul who was still assessing the rescue options by the hole.

'Well, what brings you guys here so quickly? We've only just put the request in. Are you telepathic?'

'No, we were just returning to base when we heard your call. So what we got Paul?' the newcomer asked, gazing into the hole.

The fire chief gave the newcomer a quick update. 'Trench collapse, one man trapped, but still alive.'

'Have you made contact?'

'Yes. He's got a mobile but it doesn't appear he can use it…but he can respond by tapping on the ladder. So communication is difficult.'

'Is there any way of getting a pipe or something down to him?'

"Yeah. We were just going to start putting some air down to him. There's a gap by the side of the ladder there. Look.'

'Good. I was thinking of something else.'

'Such as?'

'If we can get an optic fibre camera, phone or microphone down to him, we can better assess his situation.'

'This is why we need you with your specialist stuff.'

'Ok. I'll just brief the team and be back asap.' The Rescue Team chief made his way quickly back to his team and briefed them. They immediately jumped into action and started unloading the necessary gear.

Frank's spirits rose as the end to his incarceration appeared to be in sight. But the bad air and increased pressure on his chest was making him feel even more light headed.

Unable to take deep breaths, he was on the border of consciousness when he became aware of something clanking down the side of the ladder sending small showers on dirt on top of him. Suddenly, a small beam of light probed the blackness.

He heard a hissing noise. His oxygen starved brain equated the noise to a snake and he went into a mild panic. Trapped as he was, he struggled to move his face away from the source of the hiss.

Then a voice above informed him, 'FRANK, WE'VE LOWERED A PIPE DOWN TO YOU WHICH IS PUMPING COMPRESSED AIR TO HELP YOU BREATHE. ARE YOU STILL WITH US?'

Clank, clank.

He relaxed as much as he could.

'YOU SHOULD START FEELING BETTER,' the voice continued encouragingly.

Frank tried to take deeper breaths and noted his respiratory rate was slowing.

On the surface the rescue team had powered up the camera probe and monitor.

The voice from above informed Frank that they were also sending down a camera which had a built-in microphone to make it easier for them to hear him. He knocked the ladder twice to confirm he understood.

Slowly they threaded the probe down the side of the ladder where the air pipe had previously been fed. The operative was closely watching the ghostly image of the infrared camera on the monitor screen as it progressed deeper into the hole. Suddenly its progress into the void stopped.

'It's jammed.'

'OK. Pull it out and try again,' the Chief directed.

Underground, Frank was spitting loose dirt from his mouth as the operator tried several more times to dislodge the jammed probe, before they eventually saw something.

'Hold it there. Just swivel it around. There look, we've got an ear.'

Joe, standing nearby, stared at the monitor anxiously. 'God is it attached?' he asked apprehensively.

'Yeah, don't worry. We ought to be able to talk to him now,' the rescue team leader replied.

'*Frank, Frank can you hear me?*'

'Bloody hell. No need to shout. That's right by my friggin' ear,' Frank replied indignantly.

The Fireman quickly adjusted the amplifier volume and gave Joe the thumbs up.

'Frank are you OK?' he repeated much quieter.

'Just deaf in one ear,' came the quick reply.

'At least he hasn't lost his sense of humour,' the fireman observed. 'Frank, are you injured anywhere?'

'I don't think so. Although my leg's at a funny angle, but I don't think it's broken.'

'OK, that's good news. Before we can rescue you, we need to shore up the hole then we can start removing the earth…are you able to hang on?'

'No I'm dying for a piss.'

'Well, I think that's the least of your worries. Are you sure about any other injuries?'

'Only to my pride...can't you get a move on. What's the time?

Nearly six thirty. Why?'

'Bloody hell. I got a date at seven thirty.'

'Looking at the task we have here. I don't think you're going to make it.'

'Sod...Is Joe there?'

'Yes.' He's by the side of me.

'Can he let Liz know that I'm otherwise engaged. Tell her I haven't stood her up on purpose. If he goes through the pub, the Landlord knows her number.'

'Yes sure. He's nodded that he'll do that. No need to worry. Your love life is still intact.'

'Thanks,'

'We'll pass down a tube so you will get some water. Can you breathe alright?'

'Yeah but whoever you've got blowing air down to me, tell them they've got halitosis. It stinks.'

His comments signified a bright moment of relief. His ability to talk humorously spoke volumes for his state of mind. "Ok, we'll tell them.'

'There is one thing you ought to know though.'

'Yes, go ahead.'

'I'm leaning against a large bomb.'

'What did you say? Can you repeat please?' the Fireman requested looking puzzled. I thought you said...a large bomb.' The team on the surface looked at each other in horror.

'You heard me correctly. One of Hitler's sleepers...or it was until I tapped it with my JCB...I thought it was a pipe.'

'What do you mean sleeper?'

Every time I move, the bloody thing starts ticking. I think it's grumpy at being woken up.'

'OK Frank, hang in there,' the chief said, gesturing to the team to back away.

'I'm hardly going anywhere,' Frank replied casually.

The teams on the surface made a hasty retreat away from the hole. The camera operator joined a longer length of optic fibre cable to their link with Frank.

Frank could hear the vehicles moving.

'You guys deserting me?' he asked, concerned that he would be left alone.

'No Frank. We're just taking a few precautions and calling the bomb squad.'

Chapter 27

The atmosphere between William and Liz was tense. William was desperate to make up for his violent outburst and Liz was still not sure that she was doing the right thing by going to celebrate Frank's birthday.

She was thinking about texting him to say she couldn't make it then remembered that she had put her mobile on charge just before she went off to work at the pub.

She switched it on and it immediately bleeped with an incoming text message. She read the screen.

It was from Frank. '*Enjoyed the kiss, look forward 2 more 2nite. See you at 7:30. LOL Frank XXX*'.

She blushed and looked over her shoulder furtively to make sure William hadn't seen it. Perhaps she would go after all she decided.

'Is everything OK?' William probed, 'You seem a bit distracted.'

'No...no...it's just that when I left you earlier you were a bit...umm.'

'Down. Yes I know and I'm sorry for being such a miserable arse. I've given myself a good talking to and I'm nearly back to my usual self,' William reassured her.

She went into the bathroom.

'Do you want a cuppa before you shower?' he asked her.

'No thanks I have to meet my lift for 7:30,' she called from the bathroom.

William desperately wanted to follow her and shower with her as they normally did on his return from a tour. But he judged that he would only make matters worse so turned on the television instead.

The local news was showing a breaking story of a trench collapse, but he channel flicked and found an episode of the Simpsons and decided the light humour might buoy up his low spirits.

He went into the kitchen to make himself some tea. He heard her move from the bathroom and go into the bedroom. He so desperately wanted to watch her dress.

However, a message 'pinged' into her mobile and he thought he might have a valid reason for gaining access into the boudoir.

'Oh I suppose she will probably want to read the message,' he thought.

As he retrieved the mobile from her handbag he spotted the birthday card and the M & S bag containing the lacy black underwear.

'I wonder whose birthday?' he thought, looking at the card. It had a cartoon digger on the front and the driver was showing 'brickee's cleavage' with the words, '*nice backhoe.*'

He glimpsed into the paper bag, 'Oh nice,' he said, admiring the scanty underwear. 'She's obviously saving these for later. Perhaps I'm in with a chance after all.'

He picked up the phone and started to take it to her in the bedroom when he spotted the brief message alert, headlined on the menu screen.

Intrigued he went back into the kitchen and completely out of character he decided to search the message options. Fortunately the phone wasn't PIN protected, for, in spite of his continued nagging about safeguarding the phone with a password pin, in case it was stolen, she still failed to do so.

The sender of the message showed as '*George pub boss*'. The message read '*Frank can't meet you tonight. Will explain later. Joe.*'

William was puzzled by the message until he scrolled backwards and forwards through the list of other messages. When he saw the texts between a person called Frank and Liz, he became very angry.

'What the! Bloody hell. She is having an affair after all. The bitch.'

His hackles rose more and more as he read each message and reply. He was devastated to discover that his wife was apparently cheating on him.

His usually calm and controlled mind went into overload. In his fragile mental state he felt the pressure building in his head. He wanted to explode and race into their bedroom and confront her.

At that moment he heard her coming from their bedroom. Like a guilty child caught with his hand in the sweet jar, he wasn't sure what to do, whether to hide the fact that he'd looked at her messages or accuse her outright. He decided to put the phone back into her bag and wait.

'Oh, by the way your phone bleeped earlier. I think you had a message.'

'Thanks,' she said, as she fished in her handbag and picked up the phone. 'Oh It doesn't look like I've got a new one. It's not highlighted as being unread. Are you sure?'

'Perhaps it's from Frank.' He glared at her.

She coloured. 'Frank? Who do you mean Frank?' she bluffed, clutching the mobile to her chest as if trying to hide its secrets.

'Don't try that. You know very well who Frank is… I wasn't born yesterday. The one with the gold bracelet who unblocks drains isn't he? What have you been up to?'

Liz was flustered by the sudden exposure of her strange relationship.

'I…well…he…umm is somebody that came into our pub…and I bumped into him at the rugby club dance. I went there with Mel. Apparently he plays rugby there. There is nothing in it, honestly. He likes to chat up women that's all. He's all mouth and trousers. There is nothing going on. It's all one sided,' she rattled out nervously.

'Oh I see. So, '*Enjoyed the kiss, look forward 2 more 2nite. See you at 7:30. LOL Frank XXX*', means nothing does it?'

'It's his birthday and I…' she started to explain.

'Yes, I saw the birthday card. So was the underwear to impress him too?'

'No of course not,' she lied indignantly.

'*Enjoyed the kiss*!' he persisted. '*Frank can't make it tonight.*'

'You have no right to look at my messages,' she shouted furiously.

'Don't change the subject. If you'd have protected your phone with a pin like I told you, we wouldn't be having this conversation. And you could be carrying on with your cosy little affair and I would be blissfully unaware. Be sure your sins will find you out,' he shouted, standing up and walking towards her.

'I'm not having an affair,' she said, backing away from him, fearful that he might hit her again.

'It's a fun, meaningless relationship. It helps to break the monotony of my life waiting for you...to come home,' she shouted back. 'You don't know what it's like living with the apprehension when we hear of another explosion in Afghanistan. Is it you? Will there be a knock on my door? Will you be coming home? Look at poor Pete.'

'Don't you dare drag Pete into this...' he shouted. 'This sordid affair you've been having.' His voice became emotional. 'Pete was a great man. Not like this pathetic creature who preys on gullible service wives.'

'I'm sorry...I know how much...how much Pete meant to you. I feel sorry for his family.'

'He didn't have a family. He unselfishly decided that he shouldn't expose his family to any bad outcomes of his job...so he never got married. Perhaps I should have done the same,' William said vehemently.

'No, don't say that. We've had some wonderful times. I have always been there for you.'

'Have you? I wonder what else you've been up to when I've been away on other tours.'

'I HAVE been faithful, I promise you,' Liz said defiantly, stamping her foot to emphasise her honesty.

'Really! So this affair with this Frank is being faithful is it?' he questioned her in disbelief.

'It isn't what you think. It's his birthday and...'

'And our anniversary dinner!'

'Well I'm glad you remembered it last,' she said cynically. 'Anyway, I didn't know you'd made arrangements to go out did I? You had a face as long as a kite when I left for work.'

'What do you expect me to believe? I've just come home after a gruelling tour and it's pretty clear you don't want to spend time with me anyway.'

'No that's not true. You were the one who didn't want my company. Look at the drive home…not a word. Since you've been here, any conversation was like 'getting blood out of a stone'.'

'Shit, you know why I was like that. I've already told you. A person can only put a veneer on for a certain amount of time before the stress gets to you. I was stressed out.'

'Yes I know. I had to be brave too. Especially when you were defusing bombs here in the UK. It was even worse when you went to Afghanistan. You were not only in danger of being blown up but also of being shot…I hated that and I'm glad you're back home in one piece.'

'Anyway, this isn't about me.' William reminded her. 'This is about you and your triste…your so called harmless fling.'

'What have I got to do to persuade you…nothing is going on,' she insisted.

'And what about meeting him tonight at 7:30? So it was him and not me then?'

'Don't be ridiculous I…it was….'

Just then their home telephone rang. It stopped their argument. They looked at each other wondering who would answer it.

William glared at her and strode purposefully to the phone.

'If this is 'your' Frank,' he said, picking up the receiver, 'then I shall give him a piece of my mind.' William glanced briefly at the calling number display it showed '*number withheld*'.

'Yes.' he answered stiffly.

William listened for a few moments finally saying, 'OK. Yes of course. Repeat the location again,' he requested, and scribbled something on a notepad that Liz kept by the phone, 'I'll be there in about 30 minutes max.' He replaced the receiver.

Liz had been studying his face for any signs of who the caller might be and wondering what the message was about.

'Well, I'm back on duty. I've been called out. I'm standing in for the local EOD team. Apparently there's an incident around here. So we'll carry on this discussion later,' William hissed, and strode to the bedroom, appearing a few minutes later in his uniform.

'Are you sure that's wise in your state of mind?' she queried.

'Yes of course. I'm a professional soldier,' he said checking his uniform in the mirror.

'Pity you're not a professional husband,' Liz said quietly.

'What do you mean by that?' He turned and glared at her.

'I don't need to elaborate. I think you know,' she added, returning his look.

'It's not me having the affair is it?' he hissed. 'Is that why you need to justify it? Do you feel guilty about it?'

'No but ….'

'Well you bloody well should be. If I…' he stopped himself saying anything else. For although he was tempted to plant the seeds of guilt on her should things go wrong, this was not right.

To do so would be to introduce a negative attitude to his work and court possible failure. A deadly cocktail.

He always approached a job with a 'can do' attitude and so far it had worked.

'I need your car,' he added curtly.

'Yes, yes that's fine. The keys are over there,' she said pointing at the windowsill. 'Are you sure you should be going after all you were saying about your nerves?

'Oh so now you think about me do you? Yes of course. I have a job to do.'

'Just be…be careful,' Liz whispered miserably.

William grabbed the car keys and left, angrily slamming the door.

Liz picked up her mobile and studied the latest message 'Joe?' she said to herself. 'That's not the Landlords name. I'd better call George and see what this is about.'

PART THREE

Detonation

Chapter 28

By the time William arrived at the site, he was calm and in work mode. Years of practising Tai Chi had provided him with the ability to shut out the problems of the world and restore his inner calm. Their row had been locked away in a corner of his mind and he was now fully focussed on the job in hand.

Quickly he made his way to the Fire Chief wearing the white tabard bearing the words 'Incident Commander'.

After cursory introductions, William repeated what he'd been told on the phone. 'I understand we have a man trapped in a collapsed hole next to a suspected world war two ordnance. Is that correct?'

'Yes.'

'How is the casualty?'

'Ok at the moment. We've got an air supply going down to him and he sounds in reasonable spirits.'

'OK. Before my team get here, tell me what's in place.'

'The police have set up a five hundred metre cordon and evacuated the nearest row of houses,' the Fire chief advised him.

'Good.'

'We have communications with the man and an infrared camera which is currently stuck on his shoulder.'

'So you've not been able to see the suspected bomb yet?'

'No, that's right.'

'Well, we're going to have to dig a blast wall around the excavation.'

'There's a JCB on site.'

'Good news. Our armoured one is on the way but we could do with getting it done as soon as possible though. Have we got keys?'

'Yes and a driver.'

'Right. Lets have words with him and get that underway.'

The pair walked over to Joe, who was pacing backwards and forwards constantly checking his watch. 'Christ, can't they get here any faster?' he'd demanded anxiously.

'Hi, this is Joe the owner of the JCB. Joe this is Captain Witherton EOD.' The incident commander introduced.

'EOD?' Joe asked, puzzled.

'Explosive Ordnance Disposal,' William informed him.

'God, are you the only one coming?'

'No, my team are on their way. In the meantime, we need to put up some protection before we start even contemplating doing anything in the hole.'

'Such as?'

'Building a four foot high mud wall all around it to divert the blast when we blow it up.'

'Blow it up! Christ I hope you get Frank out before you do.'

'Of course, we'll do our best.'

'OK. Well, I'll do the wall. I can do that.' Joe said just wanting to occupy himself. 'Just tell me where you want it?'

'Fraid I can't allow you to do that. It's far too dangerous if the bomb goes off prematurely.'

'For Chrissake. He's my mate. I need to be doing something. This waiting is driving me around the bend.'

William thought of the options and agreed, 'Ok, I suppose you could start before our armoured one arrives. You realise you're doing it at your own risk?'

'Yes, OK. No problem,' Joe confirmed quickly. 'Anyway how long before your own arrives?'

'It's coming with a police escort I'd say about another 45 minutes.'

'Christ, I'll have the job done by then. Just show me where you want it and I'll get on it.'

William showed him the extent of the area he needed.

'So when are you going to get my mate out?'

'We need to reassess the situation first.'

'Reassess the situation! And what more do you need to know? There's a bleedin great big bomb down there.'

'Calm down. This isn't helping.'

'Calm down, calm down…don't you tell me to calm down. My mate is either going to suffocate or be blown sky high any minute and you tell me to calm down…for Chrissake. How can anybody remain calm?'

'Sorry, I appreciate your frustration but we need to ensure that we don't jeopardise the rescue effort and…'

'For fuck's sake just do something.' Joe climbed in to the JCB and started building the wall around the hole as directed just as the bomb squad arrived.

William quickly briefed them about the situation and as one of the team went to relieve Joe of his digging duties, William and his number two Smithy, went to the monitor screen which the Fire and Rescue team had already set up.

Joe reluctantly climbed down from the JCB and let the army man take over the digging duties.

'Why the hell didn't they fly here? Surely a helicopter would have been quicker?' he asked the Incident Commander.

'They reckon by the time they'd transferred their equipment into a helicopter they'd be here anyway. Apparently it's a relatively short distance. Same time, no advantage,' the Fire chief advised him.

'If you say so,' Joe said, unconvinced. 'So what are you going to do now?'

'We need to work with the EOD team and they'll let us know what they want us to do.'

'Well, while you're looking after your own ass, my partner is playing nurse maid to a ton of explosives,' Joe continued, irritated by the delay.

'Just calm down. You getting up tight isn't going to help your mate,' the Fire chief coaxed calmly.

'Well you don't appear to be.'

'The longer we spend talking to you, the less time we have to do anything for your partner. Now unless you calm down, I'm going to get the police to escort you off site.'

'I ...Jesus...OK, but please do something,' Joe said, exasperated by the delay.

'I repeat, we'll have to wait for the Bomb Squad to tell me what they have found...Where are you going?'

'I'm going to talk to them myself.'

Joe made his way to the monitor screen where the bomb disposal team were talking to Frank.

'Can you at least tell me what's going on?' Joe demanded from William.

'Hello. Well we've established that it is likely to be a bomb.'

'As if we didn't already know that.' Joe added cynically.

Ignoring his cynicism, William continued, 'it's not ticking at the moment.'

'So what does that mean?' Joe demanded irritably.

'It means just that, it's not ticking. There's no way of knowing how much time the detonator has used up…It's like an old watch. You shake it and it will start again but you don't know how long it will go before it stops.'

'You mean it could go up any moment?

'Yes, and it's only a short time I'd imagine.'

'Shit! The guy has been down there for hours now. Can't you move faster? Joe implored.

'It's no good rushing into this…it ain't going to go away. Now if you'll excuse me, I'll get my team to start getting the equipment deployed.'

'Do you mind if I speak to my mate please?' Joe asked.

'No, go ahead. You'll need to put the headset on though.'

'Ok, thanks.' Joe did as directed and spoke quietly into the headset microphone. 'Frank, can you hear me?'

'Yeah,' he said wearily. 'Is that you Joe? What's keeping the buggers?'

'They're building a bit of a mud wall using your JCB.'

'A wall, whatever for? Tell 'em to be careful with my JCB,' Frank interrupted. '… it ain't paid for yet.'

'I'm sure they know what they're doing.'

'Why would they want to dig a wall for Chrissake? Why aren't they getting the shit off me to get me out?'

'It's a precaution.'

'Precaution for what?'

Joe wished he'd never started the conversation. 'In case…in case after… they've got you out and…they have to blow the bomb up in situ,' he lied.

'Well so long as they don't blow it up with me next to it.'

Joe swallowed hard at the thought.

William re-joined Joe and picked up a second headset.

'Hi Frank. My name is William I am the Ammunition Technical Officer with EOD and I am responsible for defusing your friend down there. However, first I need to try and find out some more about the bomb. What does it look like?

'It's too dark down here, I can't see anything, apart from my life rushing in front of my eyes.'

'Are you able to move?'

'A bit. The ladder stopped a lot of shit falling in on me. It's created a bit of a void underneath me.'

'OK. Well we'll pass a light down so you can see better…and we'll start gently moving some dirt out of the hole by hand.'

'About bloody time too,' Frank said, relieved.

'We can't rush these things, I'm sorry…'William apologised. 'The next thing is figuring out how we can start clearing the mud without putting more pressure on the pile.'

'What about using the bucket of the JCB?' Joe suggested.

'No, my guys are using it to build the wall. We've got a special harness that we can suspend somebody from the boom of the Rescue unit or a tripod.'

'How long then?' Frank asked hopefully.

'Soon...The trouble is I'm told the side of the hole keeps collapsing...'

'Yes, it's pretty unstable as I found out to my cost.'

'We've got to move the tender closer or we set up a tripod so we can suspend one of our team over the top to start removing some of the earth.'

'The tripod sounds a safer bet,' Frank agreed. 'I've got all the mud I want down here without adding to it and having a fire tender for company.'

'So what we're going to do is pass a light down to you so you can see and hopefully feed information about the bomb back to us. But first we need to make some space for the light to go down.'

'I'll need to dig some more space around me so I can move my head and see it then.'

'OK, be very careful. We don't want to excite your companion.'

'Don't worry. I shall be extremely careful.'

'We need to identify the bomb and what sort of fuse it's got as soon as possible.'

'OK. But it's pretty tight down here.'

'We're also checking the bomb records to see if we can narrow it down that way. Remember. Any fall of mud at the wrong time and we'd all be scattered across the site.'

'Tell me something I didn't know.'

Chapter 29

The team on the surface were working frantically to get everything in place to make a safe rescue attempt, but for Frank the time dragged on with no visibility of progress and no change to his dreadful situation.

'What's keeping you buggers?' Frank groaned.

'Sorry Frank. We're just getting the tripod in place and suspending the boss over the hole,' Smithy informed him.

'I've had enough now. Just get me out of here.'

'Yes, I appreciate that. Just hang in there. We've moved some more dirt from around the ladder and hopefully we'll be able to get a light down to you.'

William's voice broke in to the link. 'Hi guys can you hear me?'

'Yes,' they chorused.

'Right Frank. Tell me when you see the light…and I'm not talking about religion here.'

'Steady on. That sounds like the mud falling on 'sleeping beauty' here.' Frank cautioned.

'OK. Steady as she goes.'

The EOD officer continued to thread the flexi cable with a new camera and light down towards Frank.

'Should be down now, can you see it?' he asked, his voice slightly strangulated by the harness suspending him.

'I saw the light to start off with, but it's gone off. Is it still switched on?'

'Yes. It's obviously gone the wrong way. I'll pull it back and try again…damn.'

'What's up?'

'Don't worry. It's stuck for a second.'

Another small avalanche cascaded down rattling off the bomb's metal casing.

'Well done. You've started the bomb ticking,' Frank informed him sarcastically.' Christ they called me a clock watcher but I didn't think the alarm would be quite so big.'

'Sorry pardon. Ah that's got it,' William said, pulling the jammed cable free.

'Aren't you going to retire to the safety of your shelter?' Frank asked cautiously, hoping that the rescue was not going to be postponed yet again.

'No Frank, I think we're in this together. Tell me when it stops ticking,' he said calmly.

'Thanks Pal, whoever you are, for not deserting me.'

'That's my job. Although I'm sure being suspended like a puppet on a string wasn't in my job description.'

'What if I bang it?' Frank asked.' Perhaps it'll stop then.'

'Probably with a big bang too. No I wouldn't recommend it.'

'Well it's going to…Oh! It's stopped by itself,' Frank said joyfully. 'Thank Christ for that.'

Well, do you want the good news or the bad news?'

'Right now I could do with some good news.'

'Ok. The good news is. The timer mighty be faulty.'

'And the bad news?'

'The ticking normally stops before it explodes,' William informed him lightly.

'Thanks for that. I'll guess we'll find out in a minute then,' Frank said sarcastically.

William continued his task without pausing to find out. 'Ok I'll try passing the light down again. Now don't worry, here it comes.'

'Yes, I can see the light again…it's still on. It's still on. I can see it out of the corner of my eye. God that's bright.'

'Your eyes will soon get used to the increased lighting. I'll just swivel the light around so it's not shining in your eyes though.'

'Thanks, that's better.'

'Can you help by positioning the camera so we can see the markings on the bomb?'

'I can't see a camera.'

'It's the small round cylindrical thing on the end of the flexi wire.'

'No I can't see it.'

'Ok. Rather than waste time, can you to tell me the details that you can see of the bomb.'

'It's a bit difficult to move without knocking against it.'

Frank wriggled his shoulders and scooped away more dirt, feeling more mud going up underneath his fingernails. He could see the bomb clearer now.

'OK. From what I can remember before the world fell in on me, It's about five feet long and thirty inches round. It's some sort of metal…but it's not rusty…it's shiny where the bucket of the JCB caught it…there's a few dents.'

'OK. Can you see the nose or the fin?'

'The nose is slightly sticking out where I must have disturbed it.'

'Is there a small propeller or gearing on the nose?'
'No…it looks like a tube. It's filled up with dirt.'
'OK. What shape would you say it was?'
'Umm…bomb shape?'
'Yes OK, but is it bulbous? Does it balloon at any point…near the middle, the waist?'

'Well yeah I suppose…but it's not the sort of waist I spend my time admiring. Hang on there's some writing on it…I can't quite read it.' Frank said straining his neck to get closer.

'What sort of writing? Is it inscribed on a cover plate…or what?

There is a moment of silence. Frank is staring wide eyed at the bomb.

'Frank…Frank are you still with me? William called, alarmed that he had lost his man.

Frank failed to respond.

'Frank, can you hear me?' William repeated with greater urgency.

'I'm…yes I…shit…Oh my god! oh my god!' Franks frightened voice had gone up several octaves. 'You've got to get me out, now.' Frank was clearly panicking. He was desperately trying to scramble out and banging against the ladder as he did so. His frantic struggle was knocking dirt on to the bomb. 'Get me out of here. Get me out for fucks sake,' he shouted hysterically.

'Frank, calm down…Frank, now listen to me,' William instructed him firmly. 'Frank, calm down or you'll send both of us in to orbit. What's the matter? What's happened?'

'Get me out…God, oh God,' Frank sobbed.

'Frank, calm down,' William repeated softly. 'What's the matter? We were doing so well…just be patient a bit longer.'

'Please...please get me out,' Frank pleaded desperately.

Smithy who was still monitoring the interchange breaks in to the link.

'Everything OK Boss?'

'No, I think he's finally flipped. He's been great up til now. A real Mr Cool, but I think it's finally got to him.'

'What's gone wrong do you think?'

'Don't know...but his thrashing around is going to trigger that bomb if we aren't careful,' William suggested.

'Are you going to pull back?' Smithy asked.

'No...no not yet...Frank...Frank. Can you hear me? Now calm down. You're doing just great.'

'Is this some kind of sick joke? Dear God! The writing...the writing...It's in German,' Frank babbled.

'Yes, the bomb loaders often used to write messages on the bombs. We used to do the same. Nothing unusual in that. Not that I usually see too many after I've dealt with them,' William informed him. 'Can you read it? What does it say?'

Frank read the two sentences in fluent German. *Alles Gute zum Geburtstag Frank. Ich hoffe, dass Ihnen meine kleine Überraschung mögen.*

'Do you know what it means?' the other asked.

'Yes, my family come from Germany. My father came over here after the war.'

Frank paused again trying to get his brain around the message.

'Frank, what does it mean? My school boy German is appalling.'

'It says...it says. Happy Birthday Frank. I hope you like my little surprise.' Frank's voice quivered as he read it.

'Wow, that's a bit of a coincidence isn't it? That your name is Frank.'

'Even greater. It's my birthday today,' Frank volunteered.

'Oh I see,' William replied thoughtfully. 'Hope you're not superstitious?'

Frank had gone numb. He just stared at the writing.

Smithy interrupted calmly. 'Boss, I gather from our bomb records that this was probably dropped on 1st June 1944 by a captured British Halifax...I believe they were after the Jet engine development that was in progress here.

Frank Whittle was the instigator of the jet engine development and coincidentally it was his birthday too.

So that's probably who the message was aimed at.'

'There you go Frank. As well as defusing bombs, we also give history lessons. See. Purely a coincidence,' William added lightly.

'Yes, but you don't understand. It's signed by Franz Schmidt. That's my Grandfather's name.'

'Just another coincidence I'm sure. Like Smith in the UK. Schmidt is a very common German name.

Chapter 30

Joe wandered over to the Bomb Disposal man monitoring the conversation between his officer and Frank.

'How they getting on?' Joe asked nervously.

'A bit of a delay at the moment Sir. But don't worry, everything will be OK,' the soldier informed him.

'Are you sure?'

'We've got one of the calmest experts out there. He's had a lot of experience dealing with these old German bombs as well as the new breed of bombs in Northern Ireland and IEDs in Afghanistan.'

'If he's so good, why is he so slow then?'

'It takes time. You can't rush these jobs. Your mate's in safe hands I assure you. If anybody can sort it it's the boss. I've seen him in some dicey situations where he was exposed to snipers and remote controlled IEDs but he never even broke out in a sweat. Ice cool he is... we call him the Iceman.'

'I wish I could be so bloody calm. How much longer for Chrissake? I don't know about Frank but I don't think I can take any more suspense.'

'Appreciate your concern. But we need to suss out the type of bomb first.'

'I know that but...does it usually take so long?'

'As I say, you can't rush these things. Believe me… he's in safe hands.

'I just wish there was something I could do…' Joe said helplessly.

'You can. Go and get me a cuppa from the catering van if you like. That would be a great help.'

Joe wandered off to the catering van and suddenly remembered Frank's request to phone his 'date' to let her know he was otherwise detained. He thought he ought to check with the pub landlord if he'd sent the text.

Joe took out his mobile and attempted to call the pub three times before he got a signal. When he got through, the Landlord told him that Liz had received the text message.

She had called him back and she had been horrified to learn of Frank's accident. George promised her that he'd get Joe to call as soon as there was any further news.

Liz hadn't initially tied Frank and William's events together. It was only when she saw the news that she realised William's callout had been to rescue Frank.

She had a dreadful feeling of impending doom. She slumped on the settee wondering whether to go to the site or wait at home.

Chapter 31

'Ok Frank. Now take a deep breath. William continued his gentle mantra. 'We can see this through together. There's nothing sinister about the message. It's just a coincidence. The bastards were always leaving messages...I think it was the Yanks that started chalking messages on bomb cases.'

'I've really had enough now,' Frank said weakly, his voice now lacking any positivity. 'You've got to get me out.'

'Just bear with me. Give me that description again,' William encouraged.

'Christ I don't know. It's a frigging bomb...It's bomb shaped,' Frank said, exasperated.

'Did you say it looked like it had a waist?'

'Waist. Girth. Spare tyre. Whatever you like to call it...Can't you get a move on?'

'We need to identify it before we even think about moving you or it... If we move it, even slightly, some bombs have gyros fitted that trigger the detonator and make a bit of a bang. ...There's no going back for a second try, if we make the wrong call. Do you understand?' William asked.

'Yes, but please hurry up. Please,' Frank pleaded.

'Any ideas boss?' Smithy quizzed, from the safety of the monitoring point.

The officer switched off the comms link to Frank so that he could speak confidentially to his number two.

'Not at the moment. As you can see, the camera isn't working and I have to rely on Frankie boy to give me the description.'

'Oh! Difficult then.'

And he ain't coping too well at the moment… I guess it's understandable when you're babysitting a testy 1000 pound bomb. Have you been able to trace any more about the history of the site yet?'

'Yeah. Apparently this was a World War two aircraft production site for Hurricanes and Typhoons. They were also developing the jet engine for the Meteor, the early jet fighter.' Smithy told him.

'Oh and therefore, a site of special interest that our 'friend' Adolf would make sure was disrupted as often as possible.' William added. 'OK. So if it was happening then what bomb types did Herman have in his cupboard?' William quizzed.

'There was the usual high explosive stuff. But their favourite on this type of target was incendiary oil bombs,' Smithy recounted.

'As I recall, they got a bit crafty with firing and anti-tamper mechanisms too, didn't they?' William said scanning his memory.

'Do you think this might be one of them?' Smithy probed.

'See what else you can get from the German authorities on a raid around here.' William instructed.

'OK.'

'In the meantime, I think we might be preparing for a hasty evacuation if things go wrong.'

The officer switched his radio system back to communicating with Frank.

Frank heard the click. 'You still there? Hey, somebody speak to me.'

'Yes Frank. Just checking with the backroom boys to try and get the low down on your friend down there. Has it been ticking again?'

'No. But if I get out of here…'

'Correction,' William said interrupting, 'WHEN you get out of there.'

'I'm never going to buy another frigging alarm clock ever,' Frank continued.

'So what have you got planned for tonight when we get out of here?' William sought to take his mind of his current situation.

'Oh I don't know. At least a few beers to celebrate my birthday to help me forget about this shit. And if I'm lucky a bit of 'how's your father' with my date.'

'Good for you. Let's hope we can get you out before closing time then,' William added.

'I hope Joe got hold of her or she'll think I've stood her up. That would really piss her off and blow my chances.'

'Oh, I think she'll know all about it by now,' William informed him. 'We've got the worlds Press and TV companies setting up all their satellite gear out here. You're world famous.'

'Can you make sure Joe got the message to her please,' Frank requested. 'Although it's probably too late now if he didn't.'

William was happy to do anything to keep his mind off his present circumstances if it kept him calm.

'Yeah sure. What's her name?'

'Liz, she's got long ginger hair and legs that go up to her armpits. She's well fit.'

Suddenly alarm bells started ringing in William's head. Surely this was too much of a coincidence. He's called Frank and his date is Liz. She has ginger hair too.

William's stomach churned. His physiological control mechanism meant he normally had full command of tensions and feelings of angst.

'I met her in a pub just across the road,' Frank continued. 'She brightened up my day.'

'Oh, what pub is that?' William asked cautiously.

'The Flying Machine.'

The information was like a knife piercing William's heart. All his primeval defence mechanisms were triggered. His mate was being courted by another male. Like a lion defending his harem, he wanted to attack this intruder and remove the competition.

'In a blind rage the Iceman tore off his headset and released the harness. In doing so landed heavily on the pile of mud that he had been so careful not to disturb. His impact sent a cascade of soil down on top of Frank.

Frank winced at the thud on the mud pile above him and was fearful that the bomb was going to blow.

Chapter 32

William stormed back to the command centre. Smithy was surprised to see him.

'Boss, what's up? he asked, concerned. 'Is it about to blow?'

'No but I am!'

'Why? What's the matter?'

'That bastard is screwing my missus,' William seethed.

The soldier looked at him in astonishment. 'What! How do you know he's porking your wife?'

'He's just asked me to get a message to her at the Flying Machine. She was his date.'

'Oh shit!' Smithy exclaimed, taking his headset off.

'Now can you see why I've left him?' William said, his face white with rage.

Their dangerous occupation had created a special trusting bond between William and Smithy. So William's revelations about Frank and Liz had made him angry too. Smithy, too, wanted to hurt the man who had offended his comrade.

'That's it. He's on his own,' William said pacing back and forth.

Smithy's mind was in turmoil. As much as he wanted to punish Frank for his liaison with Liz, he also knew it was not the right thing to do.

'Appreciate how you must feel boss. But you can't leave the poor bastard to blow himself up. Not without at least giving him a fighting chance,' Smithy counselled.

'No. I'm not going to put my life on line for a cuckold that's been screwing my wife.' William was adamant.

'Boss, you're a professional. This is what you do,' Smithy reminded him.

'Professional be buggered. I'm also a human being. I got feelings as well.' Williams anger was unabated.

'What about the reputation of the regiment if the press find out you left him?'

'Don't try that one. This is personal,' William spat.

'OK, I can understand that. I'd probably feel the same.' Desperately aware that William wanted revenge Smithy suggested, 'Look we can teach him a lesson after we get him out.'

'And risk my life getting that lowlife out of his hole. Forget it.'

There was a pause in conversation as Smithy desperately looked for an alternative.

'OK Boss, I'll do it then,' he volunteered. 'I've done a few on training exercises.'

'No, you're not going to risk your life for a shit-face like him. I can't have your death on my conscience as well. One is enough.'

'Boss?' Smithy asked, puzzled.

'Pete.' William added quietly.

'Come off it. It wasn't your fault. Don't beat yourself up over his death.'

'Let's not go over that again,' William demanded. 'I've re-lived it enough times.'

'We'll have to call another team in then. We can't expect to get a positive outcome out of this while we have negative attitude to getting him out,' Smithy repeated the mantra that William had often recited.

'And how do you think that would go down at HQ?' William said, desperately trying to think of an alternative solution.

At that moment, another soldier arrived with a piece of paper in his hand.

'Boss, we've just received this message from HQ,' the soldier announced and proffered William the note.

The officer turned his back and said, 'At the moment I couldn't give a damn.'

The soldier, surprised by his officer's response, looked at Smithy who shrugged his shoulders. 'Ok I'll take it thanks,' Smithy said taking the note and the other left confused by his reception.

Smithy looked at the note and said urgently, 'That thing is likely to have only a ten second fuze timer on it.'

Chapter 33

In the hole, Frank had been alarmed at the impact of William landing on the pile of mud, expecting any minute for the bomb to explode. He was now very frightened and frantically calling.

'Hey, you up there! Jesus Christ, he's pissed off again. Hey you bastards…Can you still hear me? Hey, I want out now. I really can't take anymore. God, what have I done to deserve this shit? Hey, please get me out before I go mad.'

In the meantime, after talking it over with Smithy, William had taken a few deep breaths and regained his sense of purpose. He realised that there was no alternative to him getting Frank out. His fit of pique now under control, he returned to his position by the hole with a plan.

He put on his headset again. 'I'm sorry about that, but I'm back now,' he announced. 'I just had to get a bit more information…You OK?' he forced himself to ask, suppressing any malevolence in the question.

'No, I've had it now…you got to get me out before I go mad,' Frank pleaded pathetically.

'Ok, but insanity is not permitted,' William advised him flippantly. 'So here's the plan of campaign.'

William disconnected his link back to control. This was going to be between the two of them, and he didn't want his conversation added to the recording of the defusing of the bomb.

'Ok...but just get on with it.'

'This woman...'

'What bleedin' woman?' Frank queried, puzzled.

'The one you want me to get a message to...'

'Liz, yeah. Is that where you went? Cos my boss was going to do it earlier.'

'No, I didn't go to play cupid. Quite the contrary actually.'

'So what's she got to do with getting me out of here?'

'Everything.'

'What you on about?' Frank demanded, suspicious at the direction of the conversation. 'Are you going to send her down here to take my mind of things? 'he added flippantly.

'No. Listen and listen good.' William's voice had now taken on a threatening tone. 'DON'T INTERRUPT UNTIL I'VE FINISHED, ALRIGHT?'

'Ok you don't need to shout. I can hear you.'

'Right...if I...when I get you out of there...you don't see her again...do you understand?'

'What! Are you mad? I'm sat on a friggin' bomb and you want to talk to me about who I'm dating!'

'Listen...the sooner you agree to what I'm saying, the sooner we'll have you out of there. Do you understand?'

'Yes, OK...ok...go on then...but hurry up.'

'The woman you're seeing is...my wife.'

'What?'

'Liz is my wife.'

'Oh shit, that's all I need,' Frank said helplessly. 'A jealous husband with his finger on the trigger. I...I thought you'd ...you'd split up with her,' he lied.

'No. I've been in Afghanistan risking my life. Not going around bedding other people's wives like you. You lowlife scum. Now listen and listen good. Your life depends on your answer.'

'Ok...OK. I'm listening,' Frank said fearfully.

'Promise me you'll never see her again...'

'YES. Anything you say,' Frank interrupted.'

'Otherwise I'll break every bone in your effing body.'

'Yes OK. I understand. I promise, alright? Now please just get on with it...'

'I mean what I say. If you continue seeing her you'll wish you'd died. DO YOU UNDERSTAND?' William said malevolently. There was no doubt as to the genuine intent of the threat behind it.

'Yes. I'm sorry it won't happen again,' Frank said fearfully. 'In any case, I've never dated her before tonight,' he started to explain, hoping to placate William. 'We were only going to...'

'Pal, I don't want to know what you had in your lecherous mind...in fact, I don't even know why I'm giving you this chance. I should just blow the bloody thing up right now with you down here.'

'Come on. Hey...I promised...that's what you wanted wasn't it?'

'People like you make me sick. Why should I believe you? I bet as soon as you get out of that hole...you'll forget about all this and be getting in to her knickers.'

'No I won't. I've already promised you,' Frank grovelled.

'No. Forget it. Why should I give you the chance?' William hissed.

'Look. I don't know what I've got to do to convince you…but…I'll do anything alright?'

'How can I be sure? If you don't have any scruples about shagging other people's wives. Why should I believe the word of a scumbag?'

'Believe me…because…because just at the moment I could quite willingly sign anything to get out of here.'

'Yes I know and that's what I…'

"Look…please…please get me out of here. I'll do anything.' Frank was becoming desperate. Looking to find something to force the issue he said illogically. 'What if I shook the bomb and then we'd both be history.'

'Yes of course, you could do that,' the other answered non-plussed. 'It helps to be a good runner in my business and I could be away from here. Perhaps even get out of the blast area. Whereas you'd be scattered all over the site.'

William's mind instantly went back to Pete's death and what he'd said about the insurgents. He knew he couldn't lower himself to their level and deliberately kill this man.

Frank had in the meantime inadvertently rested his arm on the bomb.

'Oh shit, I've nudged the bomb…and it's ticking again,' he informed William.

Instantly, the officer's demeanour changed. Gone was the jealous husband. The consummate professional returned. 'Alright, stay calm…tell me when it stops.'

'No it's still going.'

'Don't move a muscle.'

'Oh God…Ok…ok. It's stopped again.'

'Right. This is what we're going to do…'

Smithy suddenly arrived by William's side.

'Sorry Boss, but I think we've got a comms problem. I've been calling you...'

'Ok, let me check my connections...woops I must have pulled out the cable accidentally.' William admitted, re-plugging himself back into the line.

'OK, I'll check.'

The soldier jogged back to his position and did a Comms check.

'You receiving now, over?' William asked quietly.

'Yes. I can hear you OK,' came the reply.

'Just for your information. The bomb has just been ticking again...probably for two seconds,' the officer informed him unemotionally.

'Bloody hell Boss. By my reckoning that's about 6 seconds of the 10 seconds gone that we know about... let alone the time we haven't recorded. You ought to be pulling back.'

'Yes, I hear what you say but...'

'Come on. Nobody will blame you if...'

'No Smithy...we've got to...'

'Christ don't try and be a hero, you said yourself...'

'No, we've got a man's life on the line. Now, have you got any more info for me?'

'Yeah, your baby is probably a mark 12. It was developed towards the later part of the war.'

'Ok, tell me more.'

'It's got a reed relay arrangement in the detonation circuit. So you can neutralise the bomb without having to get your screw driver out. All you need to stop it is a magnet.'

'Great, where do I position the magnet?'

'There are two positions and we're just checking with our source which is which.'

Frank had been listening to the interchange. 'Two positions?'

'Yes, that's right. I expect Fritz was getting a bit fed up with our ability to defuse the UXBs...so he probably added a little challenge for us.

'What do you mean a little challenge?'

'Well, I suppose you could say a gamble really...they called it the 'Russian Roulette- Schalter'...'

'Russian roulette switch,' Frank said, translating. 'I know the German, but what does that mean?' he asked apprehensively.

'Defusing it is a gamble.' William said calmly.

'I don't understand. Surely they just dropped the bomb and when it hit the ground it blew up?'

'Not that simple. They all had different explosion settings. Some exploded on impact as you say, but others exploded just above the ground. Others were 'sleepers', designed at delaying attendance at a bombed site.

'All this talk of explosions isn't helping me. Can't you hurry up?'

'You might like to know that some were also aimed at killing rescuers and UXB people,' William said deliberately adding to Frank's mental anguish.

'Then there were mechanisms to make sure that they didn't go off prematurely when they were being loaded or if the plane experienced turbulence,' he continued. 'Enough of the history lesson. Please, I implore you. Get me out,' Frank grovelled.

'Imagine some of the manoeuvres they had to do to evade fighters and flak.'

William ignored Frank's pleas and continued.

'Your friend down there, we believe, has a final stage detonation circuitry which was controlled by the bomb loader.'

'So what you waiting for? Your mate said all you need is a magnet. Send it down to me and I'll stick it on the bomb,' Frank volunteered quickly.

'It's not that simple,' William warned. 'The person arming it could change the configuration of the switch to be either safe or booby trapped at the last moment. That way, even if we got hold of the circuit drawings, or somebody had figured out how to defuse it…they introduced this element of uncertainty…during the war a lot of our guys found this out…the hard way.'

Chapter 34

'Boss, they want to do an interview with you,' Smithy informed William.

'Who is they? I'm in the middle of dealing with Frank here.'

'The TV people. All the major international news stations by the look of it.'

'You can do it,' William suggested.

'It'll look better if it was done by an officer. Besides, you're good at 'batting' the awkward questions these reporters are likely to ask.'

As an intensely private man, William did not like being in the limelight or attracting public attention. But in his role as an EOD officer he had often been put in front of the cameras to satisfy the voracious appetite of news hungry international TV stations looking for an exclusive.

'Perhaps it might 'ring somebodies bell' about this type of bomb if I do talk to them. And, as we need more information about the anti-tamper mechanism, I suppose it might help,' he considered.

Frank was also privy to the conversation and pleaded with William 'Please don't leave me. Come on, I agreed to your terms. That was the deal.'

Smithy was puzzled. 'Terms?' he wondered.

'Tell you later,' William said softly. 'Frank. While I'm gone Smithy will continue getting some of this mud off you so we can get you out as soon as the bomb's made safe,' William added.

William was pleased to make the love cheat 'sweat' even more in his incarceration.

The Officer made his way to the scrum of TV reporters gathered around an encampment of cameras beyond the exclusion zone.

Microphones were thrust at him from all angles and an avalanche of questions were directed at him. Everybody was speaking at once. Unphased, he looked around the myriad labelled microphones and positioned himself in front of the ZDF news reporter. William knew that the German broadcaster Zweites Deutsches Fernsehen would offer him the best chance of getting to anyone associated with the bomb. If they were still alive.

Coincidentally, from his armchair in Göttingen Germany, a man called Franz Schmidt, was idly channel flicking and came across the 'breaking story' just in time to hear the newsreader say…*'Experts say that the bomb is probably a 1000 pound one dropped during the later stages of world war 2 by the Luftwaffe to disrupt the development of the jet powered Gloucester Meteor.*

'That name is familiar…where do I know it from?' the old man said repeating the name, 'Gloucester! Gloucester!'

'We visited there on holiday once. Remember? When we stayed at Heinz's place near Cheltenham,' his wife suggested. 'And you flew a secret mission over there didn't you?

'Oh, did I tell you about that mission?'

'Yes. Only about a hundred times. Remember while we were there we went looking for bomb craters and old deserted airfields or some other such nonsense in the Cotswolds.'

'Yes, that's right,' he recalled. 'The jet engine of course…We did a raid on the Gloucester Aircraft Company factory.'

'Oh so you remember now?' his wife said, going back to her newspaper.

'It was the later part of the war…we needed a propaganda victory to show the world we were still powerful. I remember. We reached deep into England and dealt a blow to their secret development of the jet engine.'

In the meantime, the television reporter continued, *'The 23 year old digging operative, who has yet to be named, has been trapped for over six hours now with the bomb. A bomb disposal expert is with him. I'm told we can go live to the scene.'*

'Hello, Trudi.' The screen changed to show a uniformed William standing by a young female reporter holding a microphone.

'Yes, hello. I am here with Captain Witherton, the Explosive Ordnance Disposal officer. We understand that there is some delay in getting the young man out. Why is that?'

'Yes, that's correct. We have to stabilise the bomb first. Every time he moves, the mechanism starts ticking.'

'Tell me more about the bomb,' the interviewer demanded.

'We have yet to uncover it. But he tells me it is about a metre and a half tall, seventy five centimetres round. It is black with a bulbous belly. It has a plate on it which says 'Happy Birthday…'

'*Frank. I hope you like the little surprise.*' William and Franz chorused.

'Mein Gott.' said Franz, expressing his surprise.

'How did you know that?' his wife queried, looking up from her paper.

'I commissioned the plate...because I dropped...the bomb.'

'What? No! This is too much of coincidence!'

Helga put down the newspaper and became interested in the coverage, shocked by Franz's revelation.

'*That is most unusual,*' the reporter said. '*Do all bombs have messages on them?*'

'*Very few. That's why we think we might be able to find out who dropped this one. It's obviously quite unique. Certainly in my experience,* 'William added.

'*So what are your plans?*' the TV reporter continued.

'*Well, we need to stop the firing mechanism somehow.*'

'*Is this an easy job?*'

'*No. The particular bomb we are dealing with is a special one. It's a sleeper.*'

'*A sleeper!*'

'*Yes. It is designed to explode after a period of time once on the ground. This is to cause casualties to rescue workers....very few have been successfully defused.*'

'*Why is it so difficult?*'

'*The designers introduced a special anti-tamper device to prevent defusing of these bombs.*'

'*If that's the case what are you going to do to get the young man out?*'

'*We're researching archives to establish how the mechanism can be made safe. Can I make an appeal?*'

'*Yes of course, carry on.*'

William ended the interview looking directly into the camera and said, '*Do you know anything about this bomb or anybody who can help with information about it? If so, please contact your local police and they will contact our control.*'

'*Thank you Captain Witherton. I'll let you get back to your vital mission.*'

The screen switched back to the studio.

As William made his way back to the trapped Frank he ignored the other questions demanded of him by the other frustrated reporters.

'Oh. So my bombs didn't all explode after all,' Franz said reflectively.

'You must tell them that you know something,' Helga directed.

'I...can't. I can't remember the details. It was something to do with magnets.'

'Please try to remember...'

Chapter 35

'Sir, we've managed to track down the name of the German pilot who actually dropped it.' The soldier who had delivered the earlier note advised William on his return.

'Great news. That's a start at least,' William said, encouraged that things were progressing.

'Apparently the records of the last flight of the captured Halifax were never destroyed. They didn't have time before the French resistance raided the place.'

'So we've got the answer?' William quizzed.

'No, not yet. But you'll never guess who the pilot was?'

'Adolf Hitler?' The officer volunteered flippantly.

'Not even close! It is definitely a Franz Schmidt. So it could be matey boy's Grandad.'

'What's the chances of that?' William said in amazement.

'Wouldn't it be spooky, if it was?'

'I'd say so…when do we get the detail?' William queried.

'They're trying to get his contact details now. But I wouldn't depend on it too much,' the soldier cautioned. 'There must be thousands of Franz Schmidts in Germany.'

'In any case he must be in his nineties. That is, if he's still alive,' William observed.

'Yes, he is boss,' Smithy interrupted. 'I've just checked with Frank. But if it is his Grammpy, we might be on to a loser. Apparently the old man does have memory problems.'

'You mean dementia?' Williams heart sank.

'No, I'm not sure if it's that or just old age. But he is pretty ancient.' Smithy advised.

How many decades ago if he did drop the bomb?'

'Christ, I can't even remember what I had for breakfast let alone what would have happened those many years ago.' Smithy replied.

'We have a dilemma then. Can we rely on what he says anyway?' William said cautiously.

The soldier handed Smithy a note.

'According to the latest information, there were several combinations they could use on the bomb.'

'Now we're getting somewhere,' William smiled.

'The crews developed a ditty to help remember the appropriate combination so they didn't accidentally blow themselves up,' Smithy relayed.

'So do we have that combination yet?' William quizzed.

'Not yet. But they're going through archive material to try and find it.'

'I'm not sure we can afford to wait for too much longer. Frank is close to the edge now as it is,' William counselled. 'But then again, it's too risky without that information. We need all the help we can get.'

'Can we give him a sedative or something?' Smithy suggested.

'No, I want him to be alert.'

'Look you bastards when are you going to get me out of here?' Frank croaked hoarsely.

'Got a bit of good news for you,' William informed him, refitting his headset.

'You're going to get me out of here now?' Frank said hopefully.

'No, they've confirmed the pilot who dropped it, possibly was your Grandfather.'

'See I told you. You didn't believe me did you?'

'Once we've got his details I'm going to call him to see if he can remember anything about the anti-tamper mechanism. Where does he live?'

'Gottingen.'

'OK, we'll try that then,' William confirmed.

'Well, why don't you get on with it then?' Frank demanded weakly.

'All we know is that they could use three positions. We need to find out which though. If we get it wrong… fireworks.'

'Oh shit.' Frank's already low spirits sank even lower.

Chapter 36

Liz had watched William giving his interview to the German TV station ZDF and decided she needed to go to the site. She had no idea what she would do when she got there. But her guilty conscience wouldn't let her rest.

She searched for her car keys and remembered that William had taken her car. She rang for a taxi and waited. The wait seemed an age.

The taxi dropped her off short of the site because of the lines of TV satellite trucks parked in the road outside the exclusion zone.

A Police car slewed across the road blocked her path at the taped off outer cordon.

'Can you let me through? I need to get there. I'm the wife of the bomb disposal officer,' she explained to the Policeman manning the tape.

'Sorry miss, I've been told to let nobody through. You could be anybody for all I know.'

Just at that moment she saw a nervous looking Joe on the other side of the tape.

'Joe, Joe. Here, over here,' she called.

Joe saw her waving and went to her.

'Joe can vouch for me. I need to see what's going on. Tell the policeman it's OK.

Joe confirmed that he knew her but assumed she was there for Frank and didn't realise she was William's wife. Eventually the Policeman relented and let her through.

'Is Frank out yet?' she asked Joe apprehensively.

'No. I don't know what they're faffing about at. The bomb disposal blokes are taking an age. This waiting is driving me mad. I could have got Frank out hours ago,' he moaned.

Joe led her to the incident control cabin and excused himself as he had been on his way to buy some cigarettes when she'd stopped him.

She recognised one of the EOD team and asked to speak to William.

The soldier spoke to Smithy. 'Smithy, the boss's wife is here. Wants to speak to him.'

Smithy took of his headset and steered Liz away from the cabin.

'Liz, you know we can't have personal visits when we're doing a job.'

'Yes I know,' Liz agreed. 'I was worried about him. We had a row before he was called out,' she confessed. And the man we rowed about is…'

'The trapped man. Yes we know. William found out and he is tamping mad as you'd expect. I've never known him so angry.'

'I just hope he doesn't do anything…anything we'd all regret,' Liz said guiltily. 'I've messed up Smithy. I didn't know what to do. So I came here rather than waiting at home.

'Worrying about it now isn't going to help either of them. Why don't you go and get a cuppa from the catering van. Hopefully it'll be over soon. I must get back. We're at a critical phase now. William is on his way back here. Best he doesn't see you,' Smithy counselled.

'OK. Thanks for listening.'

Liz wandered over to the catering truck as Smithy returned to the control cabin hoping William wouldn't see her.

Chapter 37

The phone rang out for what appeared to be an age. Eventually the voice of an old man answered.

'Hallo.'

'Hallo Herr Schmidt, Sprechen sie Englisch?

'Ja, Who is calling?'

Sir, my name is Captain William Witherton. I'm a British Unexploded ordnance officer. I wonder if you can help? I'm currently trying to defuse an old bomb dropped by the Luftwaffe during the second world war.'

'Yes, I saw you on the television news. We were going to call you. I am trying to remember the code we used. My memory isn't so good these days.'

'Oh, sorry to hear that,' William said, thinking the call was going to be a waste of time. 'I believe you were in the German airforce?'

'True. I was in the Luftwaffe and I dropped a lot of bombs on many missions.'

'The bomb I have to deal with has the name of Franz Schmidt on a plate attached to it. Could it possibly refer to yourself?'

'Yes, that is correct. That I remember now. Remind me where it was again?'

'It's on the site of an old aircraft factory. The Gloster Aircraft Company. Sometimes referred to as GAC.'

'GAC...GAC. That's right. Where they were developing the British jet planes?'

'Yes, I believe so.'

'Then you have the right Franz Schmidt. I delivered a string of bombs there to coincide with the birthday of your jet expert, Frank Whittle.

'Yes, so I believe.'

'It was the black humour of the Major. He thought it would be funny to bomb the factory on Whittle's birthday. So I commissioned the plates attached to each bomb with a birthday message.'

'Well they didn't all explode. That's why I'm involved.' William informed him.

The old man's eyes became distant as his memory took him back to the war years. He relayed his memories to William as he recalled them.

'It was May1944. The British were bombing the marshalling yards at Louvain Belgium. There were over one hundred bombers taking part in the raid. One of the planes, a Halifax heavy bomber was forced to make an emergency landing. Before the seven man crew could blow it up, they were captured by an SS Panzer division.'

William didn't see the relevance of this in his quest for information about the anti-tamper configuration, but hoped the old man would get back to the point eventually.

'The damage was fairly light. It was inspected by my colleagues in the KG200 the following day.'

'KG200! Who were they?' William asked politely.

'The Kampfgeschwader 200 was an elite Secret special operations unit in the Luftwaffe which carried out difficult bombing operations. We also flew captured aircraft and undertook long distance reconnaissance missions.'

"So there wasn't that much wrong with the plane.' William asked.

'An electrical failure to the fuel pumps, that's all. The engineers quickly resolved it. The plane was flown to one of our airfields and hidden from prying eyes.

There were seven of the best KG 200 people in the crew to fly covert operations in to England. We trained hard together. I myself was the pilot. We had a co-pilot, navigator, bomb aimer, wireless operator and turret gunners. The controls were difficult to learn at first. But we were the best.' The old man glowed with pride.

'Surely they'd know the plane had been lost.' William observed.

'Ah, but you under estimate the genius of the KG200. They painted a new registration number on it '

'Intriguing,' William thought. 'Anyway, the reason for my call...'he said, but the old pilot was lost in his reminiscences.

'The increased bombing activity by the British and Americans, alerted us to something big was about to happen. So we had to do something to dent British morale,' the old man continued. 'Part of the propaganda war.

On the night of 31st May 1944 we tagged on to the back of a returning bomber formation and followed them home.'

'Surely somebody in the formation would have been suspicious about a single bomber joining the group?' William suggested.

'No. Not at all. We knew the British used the Halifax for dropping agents off into the low countries all the time.'

'Yes I'd heard about these SOE secret missions.' William thought.

'Anyway we made it look realistic by getting two Messerschmitt 109 night fighters to pretend to attack us.'

'Bit risky wasn't it? What if they'd accidentally shot you down?

'No, they were firing blanks. The muzzle flashes made it look realistic though. These pilots were very brave as the British bombers had a large fighter escort.'

'So your mission was to bomb the Gloster Aircraft Company in Brockworth Gloucestershire then?'

'Yes. To disrupt the development and deployment of the jet engine.'

'You obviously weren't detected?'

'No. Of course not. We were in a British plane. We knew that they had developed new microwave radar that picked me up as soon as I crossed the channel. Although, we didn't want to allow them to see where we were heading.'

'So you flew beneath the radar? Bit risky though.'

'Quite so. Of course, there was no room for mistakes, but the Halifax was fitted with a British topographical radar device called H2S which helped.'

'Surely you'd have done better to use your very high altitude bomber, the Junkers Ju 86R?'

'No. For although it could fly to 40,000 feet, on one mission it was badly damaged by a specially modified Spitfire, but managed to limp home. So that was ruled out.'

'Why were so keen on destroying the Jet Engine development?'

'Our Military Intelligence, the Abwehr, received reports that there was a significant increase in the production of the jet engines. Our agents discovered that a squadron of Gloster Meteors powered by jet engines was planned for July that year. I think it was to be called 616 Squadron.'

'Well, for somebody supposed to have a poor memory you're certainly impressing me,' William informed him, feeling more confident that at the end of the old man's story he might get the detail he was looking for.

'I had to fly across to the Bristol Channel and follow the River Severn inland up to Gloucester to deliver Frank Whittles birthday present on the shadow factory.'

'That would have upset aircraft production if he'd succeeded.' William thought.

The old man continued. 'We then had to fly to a secondary target in the Regent area of Cheltenham to bomb the dispersal factory where the final fitting stages of the Meteor aircraft were being conducted.'

'A tricky night mission for you then?' William summarised, hoping the tale was coming to an end.

But the old pilot was now in full flow.

'No. I had taken reconnaissance photographs of the factory in October 1939, so I knew what course I needed to set for a one off bombing run on the factories.'

'I'm amazed you had done a reconnaissance as early as 1939.' William said in genuine surprise. 'Obviously your masters had big plans even in the early days of the war.'

Franz wasn't listening. He was lost in his memories. 'I had previously flown the route in a Heinkel 111 to lay mines in the Severn Estuary and made several single handed 'Pirate' raids on the Bristol Aircraft Company at Filton as well.'

'So you were pretty confident about navigation,' William interjected.

'Yes navigation was easy. The river Severn up to Gloucester was like a direction arrow pointing us to our target.

'So how many bombs were you carrying on the Halifax?'

'As I recall, it could carry a bomb load of 6,600 kilogrammes. Enough to upset Jet engine manufacturing for a little while at least,' the old man chuckled

'Yes if they'd all been on target.' William thought. For although at least one had exploded and caused major damage, bomb records showed that several had fallen harmlessly in the fields nearby, including the one that was keeping Frank company now.

'It all comes back to me now,' the old man said, as the years rolled back from his sluggish mind. 'This is the bit you want to know. The bombs were oil bombs as I recall, for causing maximum fire damage. They were 'Schlafwagen', 'sleeper' bombs with delayed fuzes, so that we could drop them at low altitude without getting caught in the blast. This helped our escape, too before the defenders realised what was happening.'

'Anti-tamper devices?' William coaxed.

'There was something special about them, if only I could remember.'

William thought cynically, 'after all that, this is where the trail grows cold.'

But the old man surprised him, 'Oh yes. In addition to the normal anti-tamper devices, these bombs had a special anti-tamper reed relay configured as well.'

'That's what I need to know. Tell me about the configuration,' William said, relieved at last that they were getting somewhere.

But Franz was now back reliving the mission, ignoring William.

'Anyway, as we approached Gloucester we sent our coded signal to our agents to provide the triangulated red lights for the pathway to the target. This was in case our X-Verfahren navigation and bomb equipment aiming was disrupted by the countermeasures we knew to be operating in the Birdlip area.'

'The reed relays Franz. Tell me about the reed relays,' William implored

'We lined up for our bombing run, the bomb aimer constantly calling in my ear. *links, links, recht, stetig, höher* to constantly correct our approach.

'They must have thought we were planning to land as I reduced speed to allow the bomb aimer to release the deadly arsenal as we flew towards the factory buildings.

In the plane, the tension was high. The defenders would already know we were in the area. We just hoped our cover wasn't blown.

There would only be one chance to capitalise on our element of surprise, for any subsequent bombing run on the airfield would bring the full might of the Light anti-aircraft guns defending it, on us. At that low altitude we would be lucky not to be destroyed by ground fire.

Although initially being too low for the heavy ack-ack guns to engage us as soon as they realised what we were up to, we would be in range as we climbed away.

Fortunately we were not challenged at all by any of the defences. They must have wondered what had hit them.' The old man chuckled again. 'I can imagine their confusion. It didn't make sense, one of their own, bombing the airfield.'

'There were of course no immediate explosions, but all bombs were primed and ready to blow.'

William interjected, 'Now, about the anti-tamper mechanism,' he persisted.

The old man ignored him again, lost in the nostalgia of being able to relive the tale.

'I got the confirmation that half of our bomb load had been released, and as we pulled away from our bombing run I opened the throttles to increase altitude to clear the Cotswold escarpment.

However, the heavy plane wasn't responding fast enough, so to gain enough height to climb clear of the steep limestone hill we had to jettison some of the remaining bombs along with our special long range fuel tank.

My heart was in my mouth as we rung every ounce of power from those engines. Finally, there was a glimmer of hope that we might make it. The nose lifted, a bit more, a bit more. Come on, I yelled. You can do this. Eventually we gained just enough altitude, although even then we still brushed the tops of the trees cracking the bomb aimer's observation bubble.' The old man's voice was tense as he relived the near miss.

'Then there was a loud explosion as the fuel tank and jettisoned bombs erupted in a ball of flames behind us. The explosions made deep craters in the woods, which still remain today.

I later saw them on a visit to the Cotswolds after the war had ended.'

'About the anti-tamper…' William probed again.

Franz was oblivious to the request by his revisit of the escape. 'The confusion caused by the sudden mission and subsequent explosion gave us time to get away. The British must have assumed that we had crashed into the escarpment because we weren't chased. I was expecting to be hunted down by a squadron of night fighters at least. But nobody challenged us at all.'

'Heavens you were lucky. And I suppose to add to their confusion by then, some of the oil bombs were going off as well,' William added. 'Now about the configuration of…'

'Yes, they caused a far bit of damage I believe, Franz continued, oblivious to William's need for brevity and timeliness.

'However, our planned trip to Cheltenham was now compromised and we needed fuel to get us home to our base in Belgium.

'So what did you do about fuel?' William felt obliged to ask, although he desperately needed to get back to the task in hand.

'We landed on a long concrete runway on an airfield at RAF Chedworth which had a few American aircraft on. We were able to pass on the information to the Abwehr.

We had made contingency plans if we had to land. We were dressed appropriately in Polish flying suits with the correct insignia and were carrying false documents.

Fortunately, even in those days, my English was good.

We told them we had just flown over from Pembrokeshire and they refuelled us with no problems... Why, they even gave us a cup of coffee and some American chocolate before we left.

So fully fuelled we headed for 'home'. Up to that point fate was smiling on us. That was until we crossed the English coast.

We gave the special 'Z' code using our enigma machine to alert our side of our return. But as we approached Belgium, the incompetent Wehrmacht opened fire on us, claiming that they didn't get our message, even though the Luftwaffe had received it and had even sent a Messerschmitt escort as arranged.

We were hit several times by shrapnel and so, unfortunately, I had to crash land the plane. The Geschwaderkommodore was furious, because KG 200 wanted to use the plane for several other special missions.

For his incompetence, the Wehrmacht General — der Artillerie was sent to the Eastern front to help stop the Russian advance. He was never seen again.

'I'm sorry to interrupt your story,' William said firmly at last. 'But there is a man trapped by the bomb. I believe he might be your Grandson. Frank Schmidt.'

'Sorry, Could you repeat that? I thought you said, my grandson Frank.

'Yes, I'm afraid so. Sorry to give you the bad news.'

'Frank! Oh no, there must be some mistake. Not Frank. My Frank. Why didn't you say so before.'

'You said these bombs were fitted with anti-tamper mechanism. Unfortunately, our records don't show any detail. I wonder, can you remember anything about them?'

'Oh heavens, my Grandson! Why, this is terrible.' The old man was now clearly upset by the revelation.

'Well umm…yes…there is an anti-tamper mechanism. But it is over seven decades since I dropped the bombs. Umm… I…anti-tamper…Let me think.'

'Unfortunately, we need to move the bomb to get Frank out and I must make it safe before we do so,' William elaborated.

'Can't you shore it up and dig Frank out without moving the bomb?' the old man suggested.

'No, we can't do that because the access to him is very limited. You mentioned earlier that some bombs were fitted with reed relays and…'

'Reed relays, yes that's it. Reed relays, of course. I remember now. But there was something special about them. Now what was it…? It is so long ago. My memory is not so good. Poor Frank. What was he doing to get mixed up with the bomb?'

'He was helping with a building survey. Is there anybody else that you think might be able to help? Somebody else we could talk to?'

'No…I'm sorry. I feel so helpless…my Grandson… why we used to play games when he came over here and sing nursery rhymes and…. '

'I'm sorry I don't want to sound rude and disrupt your trip down memory lane but…'

'No, you don't understand. That's it! The nursery rhyme was how I remembered the correct configuration for the anti-tamper switch.

'We had a ditty about the code. Now, what was it... neunundsechzig or soixante neuf. Something like that.'

'Why 69? Come on, it's probably not the time to reminisce about your sex life, with your Grandson cuddling a bomb,' William said, now frustrated by the old man.

'He is definitely losing it.' He thought. 'Sir, with the greatest respects we need to hurry.'

'Hush, I'm trying to remember the position of the magnetic safety switch. We used 69 and 99 and 66... I can't remember which was which though. The position of the magnet...if you get it wrong, the bomb will go up.'

'Yes, I'm aware of that Sir.'

The line went quiet while Franz was wracking his brains to recall what they used to sing to remember it.

'Sixty Nine's just fine
Sixty Six divine
Ninety Nines the mine.'

'How is this helping? William was getting edgy thinking of his team digging around an errant bomb that could explode at any moment.

'Will you be quiet,' the old man ordered. 'This is how we remembered the polarity of the magnets used to disarm the bomb.'

'What does it mean?'

'Sixty Nine, it's S and N means magnet one was positioned South polarity upwards and magnet two was positioned North polarity upwards.

Sixty Six meant both magnets were positioned with South poles upwards.'

'So Ninety Nine meant both magnets were positioned with North upwards? Brilliant,' William said. 'Progress at last. So which is the one we need to use?'

99's the mine, I guess.' The old pilot said.

'Thank you Sir. Hopefully the next call you receive will be from your Grandson.'

Chapter 38

William returned to the hole where his team had carefully removed some earth from the top surface of the landslip. However, the mud on top of Frank was still undisturbed because of his close proximity to the bomb.

William slipped on the headset again. 'Frank, I've just had a long and very interesting chat with your Grandad. Fortunately for you he has remembered a lot about the anti-tamper mechanism.'

'Thank God, you're back. I was beginning to think you'd changed your mind on getting me out of here,' Frank said wearily.

'No. I said I'd be back and I always keep my word. Like you will do, I'm sure.'

Frank understood the veiled threat and decided not to comment about his future intentions with Liz. Instead, he said, 'So what happens next?'

'We now know where to place magnets to 'switch off' the detonation circuit,' William confirmed.

'Yeah, but how are you going to do that through six foot of mud?' Frank queried.

'I'm not. You are.'

'Me? Why?!'

'You're the only one who can do it. Then we dig you out of there.'

'What if I cock up?'

'I think we both know the answer to that, don't we? But I know you won't. I'll be here to guide you all the way,' William said confidently, hoping his faith was not going to be misguided.

'No, I can't,' Frank blurted, now overwhelmed with the implications of failure.

'Well, if you want to spend the rest of your life stuck in a hole,' replied William stating the obvious.

'Oh…bloody hell. OK, I suppose there's no alternative.' Frank said resignedly.

'No, you're right. There is no other way,' William confirmed, glad that the discussion was short lived.

'So before I change my mind, are you going to pass the magnets down to me or what?' Frank demanded, anxiously.

'Remember there are two ways to put the magnet on the bomb,' William coached calmly.

'Yeah, SO?'

'Well, if you get it wrong, it just triggers the booby trap,' William added casually.

'Pity there's no room to pass down your body armour,' Frank said shaking.

'I don't know about body armour. Get this wrong and you'll be wearing angel's wings,' William said, adding some black humour to lighten the tension.

'Thanks for the vote of confidence. Are you sure there isn't an alternative option?'

'Well, yes I suppose. We could hope that the clock doesn't tick anymore. And gamble on the fact that the detonation mechanism is broken. But I wouldn't recommend it.'

'Oh God, what do we do?' Frank implored.

'Look. The chance of getting you out of there without disrupting anymore mud is nil,' William lectured. 'If we disturb the bomb, it's likely the gyroscope could trigger the detonation. So I believe we have no choice but to try the anti-tamper safe guard method.'

'OK. Let me have the magnets and tell me what the options are,' Frank said reluctantly.

'They're on their way down to you now,' William advised him.

Frank could hear the small package snaking its way down to him, A small avalanche of loose dirt anointing his shoulders announced its passage.

'Always knew there was something special about this bomb…it's got a magnetic personality,' Frank joked, trying to regain control over his fears.

'Nice to see your sense of humour has returned,' William complimented.

'Well, when you're staring death in the face…' Frank choked on his words. The realisation of his situation hit him hard. His stomach tightened. His hands started to shake. His mouth a desert of fear.

Frank watched the small net bag enter his field of vision and told William to 'Stop.' He carefully opened it and transferred the three magnets with some difficulty into his trouser pocket.

'Right, I've got them, along with another load of mud thanks.'

'Now don't put them anywhere near the casing until we're 100 percent sure of where to put them and in what configuration.'

'Yes OK. Just get on with it,' Frank urged impatiently.

'Ok. Now I want you to look at the bomb,' William directed.

'Yes, we are intimate with each other,' Frank announced, glibly.

'I'm not sure you know how kinky that sounds,' William observed.

'Yeah, whatever.'

'Right. If we're lucky and the bomb is lying the right way round, you should see a plate. Not the name plate. This is a different one.

'Let me see if I can…Yes, I think…Yes, I can see it,' Frank said, peering carefully at the cylinder.

'Ah, we're in luck then. Right, down by the plate there should be some marks printed into the bomb case. It's probably labelled '*Sicherheitsschalter*'.

'Yeah 'Safety Switch'.'

'Course, I keep forgetting you have a good knowledge of German.'

'I see it. It looks like it's a small cover secured by… by four screws.' Frank said straining his neck to see it clearly.

'That's what we want. It's the only bit of steel on the bomb apparently. The bar magnets that I've passed to you have a red end, which is…'

'North. Yeah I know…'

'Just checking. We don't want any mistakes at this stage. This needs to go on the left hand side of the plate with the red end towards the bomb's fin. Understood?'

'Yes.'

'Are you ready to place it on?' the officer asked.

'What happens if it starts ticking again as I put the magnet on the case?'

'Ignore it. But try to place the it carefully. Hopefully you will hear a faint click as the reed relay operates inside the bomb. That's what we're hoping for, OK?'

'OK. The trouble is, I'm right handed and I need to use my left hand to do this.'

Frank retrieved one of the magnets out of his pocket and started moving it towards the bomb case, extending his arm to full stretch exaggerated his nervousness. His hand shaking uncontrollably.

On the surface, William watched on his small monitor, Smithy having earlier manoeuvred the camera further down into the hole to help identify the bomb type.

'Steady as you go,' he encouraged quietly. 'There's no rush.'

Frank was now over the top of the plate but with six inches still to move down towards it. His arm was aching. His shoulder muscles on fire.

'If you don't think you can do it this time, just come back and rest your arm.' William coaxed.

'Yes sorry. I'm having problems reaching it because of this damn mud,' Frank apologised.

'Don't worry. Just catch your breath.'

Frank duly retracted his arm and rested it. After a few minutes he tried again, the muscles in his arm still protesting as he moved towards the plate. His hand started shaking again as he lowered the magnet.

'Careful now,' the officer coaxed, 'gently does it.'

The magnet caught on the raised part of the plate and it twisted out of his fingers sliding down the side of the casing out of his view…at the same time the bomb started ticking again.

'Oh shit. I've cocked up. Do you think I've messed up the Safety Switch?'

'Hopefully not. We'll soon find out won't we?' William said, in a matter of fact voice.

The ticking stopped as if to support his optimism.

'I've lost the magnet, sorry,' Frank apologised sorrowfully.

'Don't worry. The MOD has a few thousand.

Control, can you bring me a few more over just in case we need to replenish the stock a few times? In the meantime, Frank, do you want to try with the other one you've got there?'

'I thought I had it that time too,' Frank muttered to himself.

'Never mind. A miss is as good as a big bang in bomb disposal terms.'

'Yeah, I'll try again in a minute.'

A soldier from the support team jogged over with several additional bar magnets as requested and signalled for William to switch off his link to Frank.

'So you don't think we've deserted you Frank, I'm just switching our comms off. But I will be here and listening.'

'Ok, but don't be long.'

The Officer switched off the intercom and looked at his support man.

'Got some more information for me?'

'Yes. The old man has had a rethink about what he told you, but is really struggling to remember the safety switch sequence. He now thinks it's Sixty Nine not Ninety Nine.'

'Oh. Just as well we didn't get that first magnet on there then.'

'Apparently they swopped it around on different days of the week. He seems to think it was North and North on Mondays, Wednesdays and Fridays. Tuesdays, Thursdays and Saturdays was South and North.'

'What about Sundays?'

'That would have been Sixty Six, South and South I guess but the old man wasn't sure.

'What day would they decide was the correct day, because most missions started late at night and their payloads weren't dropped until the following early morning.'

'Apparently it was the delivery day which decided it.'

'So Franks Whittle's birthday was June 1st 1944, so that was a ...'

'Thursday, that's right,' Smithy confirmed.

'So the sequence for Thursday was South and North.'

'Let's hope he's remembered correctly.'

Meanwhile, in the hole, Frank had picked up the other magnet and was doing as he had been told, namely putting the North end towards the fin.

'Gently does it,' he encouraged himself. 'Just another inch.'

In his ear William could hear Franks self-encouragement and he suddenly broke off his conversation with Smithy and as calmly as he could, but with great urgency, he clicked on the intercom to Frank and said, 'Stop.'

'I'm nearly there now,' Frank said quietly, deep in concentration performing the intricate task.

'It's wrong. Stop what you're doing immediately. Withdraw the magnet. We were given duff information.'

Frank did as he was directed, shocked at the possibility that he had nearly and inadvertently ended it for all of them.

The officer could see that Frank was complying with his directions.

'Good man. I'm sorry about that. But I have just been informed of a day coding upon which they set the mechanism. The code we should be using is South and then North. Putting the north end of that magnet on the bomb would most certainly have taken our problem away from us with a very big bang.'

'Wow, that was a close shave. I'd got a technique going too,' Frank admitted, frustrated that his efforts were thwarted.

'When you're ready, we'll have another go,' William coaxed.

'You can use your newly developed technique to put the unpainted end of the bar magnet towards the fin.'

William watched, as Frank moved his hand, clutching the magnet slowly towards the bomb. He could hear Frank talking to himself, encouraging his own efforts. 'Slowly does it. Come on Frank. You can do this. You can do this.'

All the while his hand was shaking but he still had the magnet held tightly between thumb and forefinger. Every fibre of his being was concentrated on placing the it gently on its target.

Holding his breath for the final few inches of the journey, he tried to slow his wildly beating heart. He felt the magnet touch the plate, and satisfied that it was in the right place, he carefully let it go, slowly opening his fingers without moving his hand to ensure he didn't disturb its final resting place.

'Well done, great job. Did you hear the reed relay click?' the officer asked.

Frank let out a depth breath as he withdrew his arm. 'The only thing I could hear was the blood rushing through my head. I have never concentrated so much in all my life. God that was hard.'

'Well, now you've done one, the next one should be easy. Give yourself some breathing space for a few minutes and re-oxygenate your muscles. You don't need me to tell you this is the critical one. Let's hope your Grandfather's memory has been good to us.'

'Look, if we don't make it out…'

'Positive thinking. Don't let negativity even enter your psyche. We can do it. We will do it,' William said firmly.

'Ok. When we get out I will agree never to see Liz again. That's part of the deal, right?'

'I wish it was that simple. I'm afraid that you aren't the only problem. I am as well! ' William admitted painfully.

'You just happened to come along at a bad patch in our marriage. Tender emotions are just another one of the casualties of war I'm afraid. As much as I hate to say it, if you can make Liz happy then…well good luck.'

Frank was taken aback by William's candid confession.

William became business like again. 'Anyway, this isn't getting you out of here. You ready to try the second magnet?'

'Yes, I think so.'

'Positive thinking then. Don't forget this is …'

'North up. The red end towards the fin,' Frank recited.

'Spot on. Whenever you're ready,' William encouraged.

'Just in case it does go wrong though, I think you should go back to your team in the exclusion zone. There's no point in both of us…'Frank paused over his final words.

'What, and let you get the credit for making it safe? You'd ruin my reputation. No, we're in this together,' William said gently. 'We're in this together,' he repeated.

Frank swallowed hard, took the magnet out of his pocket, and started moving his hand towards the bomb plate.

Chapter 39

Frank placed the second magnet on the bomb gently and waited anxiously, his 'heart in his mouth'.

After a few minutes and nothing disastrous had happened, he breathed a sigh of relief. 'Thank Christ for that. I think we've done it,' he said pleased with himself.

'See, there was nothing to be worried about, was there?' William said, equally relieved.

Immediately he started digging to release Frank. The officer insisted that no-one else in his team should join the excavation until he was satisfied that the magnets were taped securely in place.

As a precaution, whilst the Officer was digging, Frank sheltered the bomb from small earth falls with the aid of a small, specially designed umbrella type device.

Stripped to his waist, it took William an hour of energetic digging to reduce the pile of mud over Frank. The task took longer than usual because he was shoring up his excavation as he dug down to prevent any further collapses.

Finally, he was able to see the hair on top of Frank's head. Carefully, he knocked through the hardened shell of the mud cocoon that had been Frank's tomb for so many long hours.

'Doctor Livingstone, I presume,' he said, thrusting his hand into the gap.

'I wondered what you would look like,' Frank said tearfully, grasping the other's hand, relieved at last to feel the touch of another human being. And to breathe fresh air again.

'Right, let's see if we can get you free of this lot then,' William said, examining the mud pile.

'I think my leg is squashed against the side of the bomb,' Frank volunteered.

'OK, I'll go carefully.'

William dug into his back pocket and fished out a squashed mars bar and offered it to Frank. 'Do you want this?' he asked.

'Yes, please,' the other replied taking it off him hungrily. 'I could murder a pint though.'

'All in good time,' William said, surveying the mud and deciding his best approach.' All in good time.'

It took William another half an hour to uncover the bomb, complete with its safety magnets.

'This is where I earn my Blue Peter badge,' he said, removing some plasticine from the small tool pouch at his side.

Quickly he surrounded the two magnets with a circular shape dam of plasticine and then gently sprayed them with quick setting foam. Finally, he used long lengths of gaffer tape to secure the complete 'ensemble' to the bomb case once the foam had hardened.

'Well, that should do it,' he said, starting to move mud away from Frank's legs.

Frank was able to help as the weight of soil was removed from his legs.

But as he did so the bomb moved slightly, and to their horror it started ticking again.

'Oh god, don't say we've got this far and now we've blown it,' William thought.

He looked at Frank briefly and then resumed his frantic digging.

'Get out. Save yourself,' Frank said desperately.

The officer ignored him and increased the pace of his digging. After 30 seconds the ticking stopped and a fizzing noise emerged from the bomb, accompanied by a small cloud of acrid smoke, which started escaping from the damaged casing where Frank had scuffed it with his JCB.

'God, this is it,' Frank said, his mouth dry.

The officer continued to dig even more frantically. 'Don't worry. It's probably only the detonator. Hopefully we've made sure it won't trigger off the main explosives…and I think the chemicals have degenerated too, judging by the wet fart noise that it's making.'

Frank could feel the warmth of whatever was going on inside the bomb conducting itself through the casing to his calf.

'Sorry to be a wimp, but my leg's getting hot,' he informed the other.

'OK, we'll just get this last bit away from your leg and you ought to be able to shuffle away from it.'

Carefully, William dug the last remnants of mud away from Frank's leg and gently lifted it from the contact with bomb. Frank cried out in pain as his trapped foot was finally released from the mud.

'Oh God! That feels painful now that I'm getting the circulation back into it.'

'Right, control, lets have the tripod manned again. I shall be ready to get him out of here in a second or two,' ordered William.

His request had already been anticipated by his team, who immediately leapt into action.

William reached into a large holdall which he'd put on the edge of his excavations and pulled out a climbing harness.

'I'm going to put you in this harness and get the boys to pull you out sharpish. OK?' William told Frank.

'I can probably crawl out,' Frank said.

'No. The guys will be here any minute.'

Even as he spoke, a rope snaked down into the hole and Frank could see the tripod above.

Quickly Frank donned the full body harness, William connected it to the rope and gave the sign to haul Frank up. As Frank was lifted out however, the bomb moved too and started to roll over.

William quickly jammed his spade against it to stop it rolling on the precious magnet assembly as Frank was rapidly pulled out of the hole and whisked away by the team. Although they were tempted to give him a rough time because of his affair with Liz, they desisted because the world's TV cameras focussed on their rescue mission.

William was now alone in the hole nursing an angry bomb, wondering how he was going to stop it rolling any further.

Chapter 40

Frank had been hastily carried away from the hole by two of the bomb team and immediately placed on a stretcher where the paramedics were waiting for him.

After a cursory glance, they decided that there were no life threatening injuries that needed to be treated on site, so they took him towards the ambulance which was safely parked beyond the exclusion zone.

Liz had been alerted to the sudden burst of activity and watched fearfully as Frank was rushed away from the hole.

As the two paramedics carried him towards the ambulance Liz ran over to the stretcher.

'Frank, Frank are you OK?' she asked, softly.

'Liz. What are you doing here?' Frank said, feeling uncomfortable after William's threats.

'I had to come to be near. The waiting at home was torture,' she blurted. 'Are you hurt?

'My legs are a bit buggered. I reckon I'll be on the subs bench for a few games,' Frank said, wearily. 'But otherwise I'm OK.'

'Oh I'm so glad you're alright. You must have been so scared.'

'Yeah, well, there were moments when I didn't think I was going to make it, I must admit,' he said, his lips a red slash in his mud coated face.

'I bet you did,' she said, holding his muddy hand. Still, you've had a mud pack that I would pay a fortune for,' she added, trying to make light of his near death experience.

'Yeah, it does feel a bit strange,' he said, pieces of the dried mud flaking off onto the stretcher as he spoke.

'It must have been awful down there?'

'To say the least, but the worst bit was finding out that the bomb disposal man was…was…'

'Yes, I know. It's my husband.'

'He knows about us,' Frank said looking at her nervously. 'I thought at one stage he was going to leave me down there.'

'Oh God!'

'Yes…Look Liz, I made a deal with him,' Frank confessed.

'A deal, what sort of a deal?' she asked suspiciously.

'If he got me out…'

'Yes.'

'I'd never see you again.'

'What! You made a deal with William. That's blackmail.'

'He still loves you Liz.'

'He's got a funny way of showing it if he does,' she said, subconsciously putting her hand to her cheek.

'Why don't you at least give it a try?'

'It's too late. We've grown apart. He's had his life in the services and I've…I've waited a long time for him. No I'm looking for something different.'

'Liz, I'm very fond of you, but…I've got to confess that I only dated you for a bet.'

'A bet!' Liz stared at him in disbelief. 'A bet!' she repeated, devastated by his crass admission.

'Yes…I'm sorry. Anyway, it wouldn't work. I'm a young guy. I need to have a few flings before I settle down. I'm enjoying life.'

'And you weren't enjoying life in my company?' she said, shocked. His words twisted a knife in her stomach. She had been a fool to think this young man would want to be associated with an older woman for anything other than sex. She had fantasised about romance, but now she felt used and ashamed.

After his ordeal, Frank struggled to find the right words.

'No, I didn't mean that… I don't want to be tied down…not yet in any case.'

'You're not just saying this because of your promise to William are you?' she demanded.

'No, of course not,' he lied.

'Frank, you made me feel alive again,' she blurted, 'I'm different. I'm happy for the first time in a long time. I like seeing you. Please don't walk away from me. Please.'

'We can still be friends…' Frank croaked.

'I want more than friendship. I want to be loved. To be touched, stroked, hugged. I want to be cared for and to care for somebody else.'

'You have William, now he's back from serving abroad,' he volunteered unhelpfully.

'I don't feel the same about William anymore. He is so…so staid in his ways. So unemotional.'

'He saved my life, remember? Perhaps his job has made him that way. Let's face it. I've seen him in action. I'm glad he's cool. You wouldn't want to get excited around those bombs.'

'No, but it would be nice if he got excited about me though,' she added wistfully.

'He's still down there at the moment. The bomb rolled over as they were getting me out. William was holding it with a spade to prevent the anti-tamper magnets being knocked off.'

'Magnets!'

'Yes. He talked me through putting them on the bomb to stop it blowing up. Something was getting hot inside and it was burning my leg. William sorted it. He was cool as cucumber, thank goodness. I hope he's alright. I owe him big time.'

'Sorry, Miss, we need to get Frank to hospital,' the lead Paramedic interrupted quietly. 'You can come to the hospital with him in the ambulance if you wish.'

Liz thought for a moment and said, 'No, it's OK. My husband is still working on the bomb. I should stay and support him. Thanks for the offer. Goodbye Frank, I'll…pop in and see you sometime… when you're settled.' She let go of his hand. Frank looked at her briefly then closed his eyes, feeling guilty for leading her on.

Liz watched as Frank was loaded into the ambulance.

She was torn between loyalty for William and the happiness she felt with Frank. They had known each other only briefly, but she had really looked forward to being in his company. It was like having a first love all over again. Frank's enthusiasm for life was infectious.

As the ambulance doors slammed, Joe came running towards her.

'Is that Frank?' he quizzed, panting.

'Yes,' you just missed him. Where have you been?

'I had to have a whisky to steady my nerves. Is he alright?' he asked cautiously.

'Yes. He's fine.'

'I can't believe after all this waiting I missed him.'

'I shall miss him too,' Liz said quietly.

Chapter 41

Liz turned back to look at where William was still working on the bomb.

Suddenly a huge fireball lit up the night sky and a plume of muddy water shot fifty feet in to the air, followed by a loud, ear-splitting explosion. Windows rattled several miles away from the noise of the blast.

The 'Snow White' bomb had woken noisily…

Liz was deafened by the explosion and nearly blown off her feet as the percussion wave hit.

'Oh my god, William!' she shrieked.

This was the moment that she had dreaded ever since he decided to be a member of the EOD team. She had often imagined the knock on the door and for the 'uniforms' to tell her about William's death, but not to be there and actually witness him being atomised.

The shock was too much for her. Her senses overwhelmed and she passed out.

She surfaced slowly through the blackness. Had she died? She felt awful. Her vision was distorted. She could make out blurry faces. There was a rushing noise in her ears. Consciousness hurt. The back of her head painful. She wanted to go back to the blackness.

'Liz are you OK?' a voice asked faintly through the buzzing in her ears.

She was afraid to open her eyes. 'What...what happened?' she croaked.

'You fainted,' the voice informed her. 'Just lie there for a bit and we'll sit you up shortly.'

She was lying flat on her back. Someone had raised her feet. She could feel a stickiness at the back of her head. As her vision was clearing, she could make out a uniform. An army uniform. Suddenly she remembered the explosion. Her heart sank.

'William, Oh my God, William!' She started to cry.

She put her hands to her face and covered her eyes, her body now wracked by grief. It was only now that she realised she still loved him. It was as if a huge chunk of her whole being had been hacked away.

Her heart ached so much that she thought she was having a heart attack. They had been together for over fifteen years and now...

People around her looked away, embarrassed at her distress, not knowing what to do or how to comfort her.

She heard someone approaching, someone calling her name. Perhaps she had suffered the heart attack and she was dead, because it sounded like William but William was dead. The bomb had exploded.

'Liz, Liz are you alright? Liz, it's me,' William said, kneeling down by her side. She opened her eyes. Was she imagining it? He was there, gazing down at her. Were they both in heaven? He touched her hand. It felt real.

He bent down and kissed her on the forehead and gently stroked her hair.

'Are you OK?' he asked, looking into her eyes.

'I...I think so,' she said, feeling light headed.

'You must have been knocked over by the blast. Sorry the bomb went off before we could warn everybody,' William apologised.

Liz sat up and touched his face.

'It really is you?' she said, overjoyed at seeing him.

'Yes, it's me. Snow White didn't like being woken up. She was a bit grumpy.'

'Snow White?'

'Yes. It was Frank's bomb,' William said, uncomfortable at mentioning the other's name. 'It must have been awful for you hearing it go off like that. Of course we're used to hearing explosions like that all the time,' William added.

'You're alive!' she exclaimed looking into his face.

'Yes. Another successful job. Although you never know with these world war two bombs,' he said flippantly.

'You saved Frank.'

'Yes. That was a bonus. She slept long enough to get him out...although it was touch and go a couple of times.'

'Yes, so I gather. Thank you. He told me that you made a deal.'

'A deal?' Oh yes. That was purely to stop him freaking out. I didn't mean it.' William suddenly looked sad, 'Liz, I...didn't think you'd still be here...I thought you might have gone off in the ambulance with...with him.'

'No, I couldn't, while...while you were still in danger,' she confessed.

'He...and you are free agents. I can't dictate how you run your life. Although I realise I haven't actually given you much of a married life,' he added awkwardly.

'But I'm glad you could see me at work and…um give you the right result.'

'Yes, you have given me the right result.' She paused reflectively, 'I realise what a stupid idiot I've been.'

'Oh?'

'There's me imagining that a young man like that would want me for myself. What a fool. Why, I'm almost twice his age. No. It's not him. What you've done is given me…you.'

'I'm not sure I follow,' he said, perplexed. 'I thought you and him…'

'There is no me and him…there never was. Will you forgive me William?' she begged, 'I realise I've been… been stupid, but can we give it another try?'

'I think you know the answer to that,' he replied, squeezing her hand. 'Now I'm home, perhaps it will be easier.'

'I thought you'd died out there,' she said quietly. 'And I couldn't bear that pain.'

'I'm sorry if I frightened you,' he apologised.

'I didn't see you leave the hole. When did you escape?' she asked.

'Well, I realised after they got him out, there was no way I could keep the anti-tamper stuff in place, so I hightailed it out of there as soon as my team confirmed that he was safely away.'

'Here. How come you've got a clean face when Frank's was filthy?' Liz asked, examining his face.

'I had a rendezvous with a damp flannel. After all, I have to look my best. I'm about to be interviewed on world-wide television,' William said, lifting her into his arms.

'Ooh, I didn't realise I was married to an important TV personality,' she said, snuggling up against him.

'I love you Liz,' William said, suddenly.

She looked into his eyes and for the first time in many years she was reminded why she'd fallen in love with him.

'The eyes are the pathway to the soul,' she recalled. She saw intensity in his gaze that made her heart flutter. It was hypnotic. 'If love was a visible entity, he was exuding it,' she thought, dreamily.

The headiness she felt meant the world and its problems were retreating in to a peripheral haze. He had become the centre of her being again.

She responded with a passionate kiss.

The small group of spectators, who had come to Liz's aid when she'd fainted, applauded. Liz and William broke off their kiss and laughed, content in each other's company.

Chapter 42

In Gottingen, Lower Saxony, overlooking the meandering River Leine, Franz Schmidt re-ran the interview with William and the bomb explosion for the tenth time.

'Do you have to keep doing that?' his wife bellowed.

'This is great. Normally, we never got to see the actual explosion when we were on a bombing run. It was more important to escape from the flak. We only saw the bomb craters from later reconnaissance photographs.

Pity that Frank Whittle never had his birthday present though,' Franz muttered, thoughtfully. 'Who knows how things might have turned out?'

'The important thing is that your Grandson is alive. That's all that matters,' his wife reminded him.

'See I told you there is nothing wrong with my memory,' the old man added, rerunning the news clip again.

'So why didn't you buy me flowers for our anniversary then?' his wife demanded. 'Don't you dare say you forgot, Franz Schmidt.'

Post Script

Fortunately the bomb had not done any damage to its original target. For having lain dormant for many decades, it had slumbered too long. Thankfully, although it failed to disrupt the development of the jet engine, the original bombing mission however had the effect of waking up the planners to disperse the development of the engine to other sites. In addition it speeded up the pace of development and use in the Gloster Meteor aircraft.

The Meteor was used to intercept and disrupt the fast V2 rockets by flying alongside and using their wing tips to knock them off course. Credit must go to the incredible skill and bravery of the RAF pilots who undertook these dangerous missions.

Today's easy global travel owes a lot to the pioneering efforts of Frank Whittle and his team of developers.

Fact Footnote: On 1 June 2010, a World War II-era British bomb exploded in Göttingen Germany while disposal teams were seeking to disarm it. The 500 kg (1,102 lb) bomb was found by construction workers building a new sports arena. The bomb was the second found in a week; the first having been disposed of safely. Three people were killed and six injured in the blast.

Also by the Same Author

Godsons – Counting Sunsets

Godsons – Counting Sunsets is a heartening story, charting the stubbornness of the human spirit to let the precious gift of life slip away without a fight to the bitter end.

Multimillionaire Geoffery Foster has been diagnosed with terminal cancer, and has irrationally swapped his luxurious Monaco penthouse for a single room in a Cotswolds hospice in Gloucestershire England.

Determined to maximise his remaining days and impressed by the selfless humanity shown by his hospice nurse, Andy Spider, Geoffery decides to redress his neglected Godfather responsibilities.

Together Andy and Geoffery embark on a journey to track down and improve the lot of Geoffery's three Godsons.

But will resolving the problems of childhood Meningitis amputee Tim, the alcoholic 'drop out' James and the abused husband Rupert, be too much for Geoffery's frail health.

Added to his challenges, a drunken and intimate wedding reception encounter with a former girlfriend comes back to haunt Geoffery as he also gambles with his life in the hands of a woman spurned.

Counting Sunsets becomes the abacus on which Geoffery records his remaining days.

Proving, 'It's *never too late to be who you could have been.*' *George Elliot.*

The Godsons Legacy

Andy Spider continues to be the glue that cements the three Godsons together as they expectantly await the release of their legacy from Geoffery Foster's will.

But surely even this pillar of society will be distracted from his task when tempted by the radiant beauty of Nadine. Mesmerised by the exotic Monaco nightlife, his stoic resolve is weakened by lack of sleep and too much alcohol.

Pallbearers wearing Basques, Murder, Blackmail, Fear, Lust, a Motorway Crash, a runaway teenager and Police Investigations are the unexpected consequences of Geoffery's legacy as he still controls their lives FROM BEYOND THE GRAVE.

The story is set in Gloucestershire England, near the beautiful Cotswold Hills

The Godsons Inheritance

The three Godsons have to work harmoniously to place the final piece in the inheritance puzzle for the release of their legacy.

But the wayward Tim makes it a challenging exercise. His self-centred, bloody-minded arrogance means the whole intricate web of relationships is jeopardised. Will his heart bring him back in line or will he still be ruled by his head?

Meanwhile Rupert is continually in fear of his vicious megalomaniacal wife; James is clinging on to life desperate for a liver transplant.

Young army veteran Carrie is haunted by the trauma of active service.

Ben a young carer for his alcoholic Mother inadvertently opens up old wounds by looking for his father. Can fellow young carer Janie help or hinder Ben's traumatic life?

Andy is having a bad time in his personal life, haunted by a late night indiscretion and frustrated by having to coordinate the activities of the three Godsons.

The story comes to a dramatic and exciting conclusion, but is it the end? In this the third book in the Godsons series.